MURDER
AT
CHIMNEY
BLUFFS

An Edmund DeCleryk Mystery

BY
KAREN SHUGHART

For information, please email Silver Waters Press at silverwaterspress@gmail.com

ISBN: 979-8-9921090-3-0

Design by Book Shine Design- www.bookshinedesign.com

Thank you to Cathy Contant and John Kucko for permission to use the photos that inspired the cover.

This book is dedicated to my husband, Lyle, who for more years than I can count has been my biggest champion, most honest critic and greatest fan, and who without fail, and daily, makes me laugh. And to Jessica, Jeremy, Debbie, Alan, Joan, Marcy and Jim. I love you all.

Author's Note:

Chimney Bluffs is comprised of several tear-dropped shaped hills called drumlins that were formed millions of years ago by glaciers and then shaped by wind, rain, snow and waves into what appear to be chimneys. This unique attraction is located between Syracuse and Rochester, NY along Lake Ontario.

"So wise so young they say, do never live long."
Richard III
William Shakespeare

Prologue One

July 1925

At 9:30 on a quiet evening in early July, a shadow boat owned by rumrunner Liam O'Connor sailed onto Lake Ontario from a beach beneath the cliffs at Chimney Bluffs to intersect three miles offshore with a schooner that had embarked from Main Duck Island, Ontario, Canada. A sliver of a new moon peeked out through gathering storm clouds as the boat ploughed through turbulent water toward its destination.

"I'm quitting, Liam; tonight's my last run. Dorothy's pregnant, and with a child on the way I can't continue to take risks like this," his brother Harry announced.

"You've made a good living working for me, Harry. Dorothy should be happy with the money you bring home."

"What we're doing is *illegal*, Liam. If we get caught, we'll go to prison. What will happen to my family then?"

"Well, don't you worry, my boy, you're safe tonight. Someone tipped off the Feds, and they're headed toward Alexandria Bay. They've been led to believe a shipment will be delivered near Clayton." Liam chuckled and winked at his brother.

"It doesn't matter, Liam. I am *not* going out with you again."

"What will you do to support your family? It's not easy to find a good paying job these days."

"Ted Fisher's manager is moving to Binghamton, I'll be replacing him at the hardware store. I won't make as much as I do now, but Dorothy's no gold-digger, we'll have plenty to live on. As I said, I can't take any more risks."

"You'll regret this someday, but don't come back to me crying if that job doesn't work out. I'll have no trouble replacing you."

The brothers spent the rest of the journey in silence. Then, about thirty minutes later, a lantern with a red light swayed slowly back and forth three times, announcing the arrival of the other craft. The two vessels anchored side by side, rocking precariously as angry waves slapped into the hulls and onto the decks, drenching the men with chilly water.

Liam and his Canadian counterpart, Etan Canersky, exchanged greetings. Canersky motioned for the brothers to climb aboard to view the bootlegged liquor.

Satisfied, Liam opened a leather satchel, displayed a wad of cash, and handed the Canadian a stack of bills. "Here's the down payment. You'll get the rest as soon as the hootch is safely stored in my hold."

With his crew of three, Canersky worked alongside the O'Connors to load the goods onto the American boat. Several minutes later, with the transaction completed, Liam handed over the rest of the money.

"Thanks, mate. Just so you know, I'm getting into another line of business. My successor will contact you to schedule the next delivery."

"Moving into management?" Liam asked.

Canersky put his finger to his lips. "Confidential, can't talk about it now. How about a little toast to celebrate my new endeavor?"

Harry, anxious to return home, said, "Liam, we've no time for this. We'd best be getting back, it's late."

"Loosen up, Harry," his brother replied. "One drink won't hurt."

He jumped onto the deck of Canersky's boat and motioned for his brother to join him. "Come on, this is your last night. Let's have a little fun."

Harry sighed. "Just one, then."

The Canadian grinned. Opening the top of a bench seat, he retrieved a large container, set it on the deck and pulled something out of an oilskin jacket that lay nearby. "Here's to my bright future."

PROLOGUE TWO

100 Years Later

July was a glorious month in Lighthouse Cove, NY: warm, sunny days with cottony white clouds floating across an azure sky, clear nights with a dense canopy of crystalline stars illuminating the inky heavens. It was a month when the air could occasionally be as humid as August or as cool as late September, depending on the angle of the sun and direction of the wind.

In a multitude of shapes and sizes, leaves on deciduous trees offered refreshing shade to heat-rippled streets and sandy roads. Tiny round orbs of ripening stone fruits, pears and apples, poised delicately on branches in nearby orchards. A profusion of bright flowers clustered in yards, edged driveways, encircled the tiny gingerbread cottage-like visitors' center, and bordered entrances to municipal parks. Sea grasses and wildflowers clung tenaciously to sturdy sand dunes at the end of weathered wooden walkways overlooking Lake Ontario.

In July boats sailed, motored, and meandered on the big lake and Silver Bay, or anchored at sandbars for passengers to party and swim in shallow waters. Beaches and playgrounds reverberated with the sounds of happy, squealing children while gulls boldly sauntered onto picnic blankets to snatch cookies, chips, or a half-eaten sandwich.

Canadians from across the wide lake settled into quaint, charming rooms at inns and bed and breakfasts to drive the scenic Lake Ontario Seaway Trail, tour historic lighthouses and sample award-winning wines produced by local vintners. Farm stands, open daily from just past dawn to dusk, beckoned passersby with colorful hand-made signs offering fresh produce, eggs, cheeses and meats, baked goods, beverages, herbs, jams, and honey.

Concerts on the bluff where the Lighthouse Cove Historical Society and Museum stood entertained residents and tourists on Sunday afternoons; folk singers delighted crowds on Tuesdays at the gazebo in the village park; bands played oldies, jazz, and country music on decks at nearby restaurants.

July was a glorious month, indeed, unless you discovered something on a deserted beach one sun-kissed afternoon that would haunt your waking hours and cause bad dreams for weeks to come.

CHAPTER 1

His alarm buzzed at 4:15 a.m. He rolled over, hit the snooze button, and fell back asleep. Fifteen minutes later it buzzed again; he turned it off and jumped out of bed.

Stumbling into the kitchen, he opened a canister of coffee and measured some into a filter. He added water to the pot, turned it on and walked to the bathroom to take a shower. Several minutes later, now dressed and ready for the day, he sat on a chair in his living room sipping from a travel mug while he scrolled through emails on his phone.

He poured himself another cup, grabbed his laptop from his desk, placed it in a messenger bag, and stuffed the phone in a pocket. Carrying the mug, he exited his apartment making sure to lock the door before walking down the corridor to the elevator that would take him to the lobby.

Noah Pierce stood outside his building, waiting. The days were long this time of year—he could see the sun coming up in the east—but the street was deserted, with only birds slowly awakening from slumber breaking the silence.

He removed his phone from his pocket and looked at the time. He'd been waiting for ten minutes. He'd wait a few minutes longer, send a text to cancel, go back inside and get a little more sleep, and later, head into work. He placed his phone back in his pocket and shifted his bag from one shoulder to the other.

As he stood and turned toward the front door of his building, a black SUV pulled around the corner and parked along the curb in front of him.

"Noah? Sorry I'm late. There was an accident on the highway."

"I was beginning to wonder when you would get here." He opened the door and with a deep sigh slipped into the passenger seat.

CHAPTER 2

The day dawned bright and clear, with a cloudless blue sky and lemon-yellow sun casting warming rays onto the serene lake beneath the bluff where Ed DeCleryk and his wife, Annie, head of the Lighthouse Cove Historical Society and Museum, lived in a restored circa 1850s ship captain's house.

A retired Navy SEAL and police chief turned criminal consultant, the tall, lanky white-haired man awakened to a raucous chorus of birdsong, walked downstairs to the kitchen, brewed himself a cup of coffee and meandered outside to the back porch with his laptop to read the morning news. Annie was still sound asleep, their petite, elderly beagle, Gretchen, snoring gently beside her.

Sipping his coffee, he sat quietly for a few minutes, observing the world awaken from slumber. A bald eagle soared on gentle currents of wind. An insect-loving, red-bellied woodpecker drummed rhythmically into the bark of a wind-bent scrub pine twisting precariously toward the water; a vigilant gray squirrel with tiny hand-claws munched on blackberries from a nearby bush, his wide eyes darting back and forth to Ed, wondering, friend or foe?

Ed felt centered and peaceful. He'd spent a quiet winter and spring working on projects around the house, reading, attending cultural events and celebrating birthdays and holidays with friends and family. He looked forward to a carefree summer.

He felt a hand on his shoulder. With Gretchen by her side Annie, a small woman with short, spiky grey hair and lapis-colored eyes, bent over and kissed him on the top of his head. The beagle nudged his leg; he scratched her ears.

"Lovely morning," she said, cradling a mug of hot tea in her hands. "How did you sleep?"

"Like a log," he replied, his smile reaching up to his pale blue eyes. "I always sleep better with the windows open instead of air conditioning. What about you?"

"I slept well, too."

"Did you feed Gretchen?"

"I did. As usual she was starving. She scarfed her food down in less than a minute."

"I was surprised she didn't wake up when I did. That's not typical of her."

"She's getting older, Ed, and definitely slowing down. I noticed she tires more quickly when we walk her, and she's been napping frequently during the day.

"I didn't hear you when you left the bedroom, either. I guess I'm also feeling my age. I'm completely exhausted after working all weekend at the museum."

"Maybe it's time for both of us to consider retiring, Annie. We could buy an RV and travel the country. Think of all the places we could go and things we could do. We could even spend as much time as we like with our children and grandchildren," Ed said with a grin.

She rolled her eyes. "And most likely wear out our welcome. Good idea, but not just yet. I've a few more years to go before packing it in."

"Do you have to go into work today? I was hoping we could take the pontoon out for a picnic lunch at Chimney Bluffs. The weather's perfect. And while the picnic area and hiking trails will be crowded, we should have the beach mostly to ourselves, considering no swimming is allowed because of the strong undertow.

"That's a wonderful idea, but I need to spend a few hours at the museum this morning working on last-minute details for the garden club luncheon at Fitzhugh House this weekend. Jason's in all day; he can cover for me this afternoon. I'll be home by lunchtime."

Jason Shipley had started working for Annie as a summer intern while in college; then after graduating , as her administrative assistant. Several months ago, he was promoted to assistant director. When she retired he would replace her.

"While you're at work, I'll take Gretchen for a walk and pack the picnic basket. I can stop at the sub shop and get some sandwiches and drinks."

"No need. We have ingredients for Provençal tuna sandwiches, I'll make them before I leave for work. There's a bag of veggie chips in the pantry, and a couple of lemon and blueberry tarts left over from the weekend. We have some bottled water in the refrigerator."

"How about some wine?"

"That would be lovely. Do we have any dry Rosé?"

"We do. I'll get a bottle from the cellar and place it in the refrigerator to chill."

"Perfect. Changing the subject, do you remember that we're meeting Suzanne and Garrett for dinner on Friday night at Rumrunners?"

Originally from Jamaica, Suzanne Gordon, tall, with ebony skin, curly dark hair cut into a stylish bob, and huge heavy-lashed brown eyes, was one of Annie's closest friends. She ran the wellness center in the village.

Her tall, handsome husband, who had dark brown hair and cognac-colored eyes, was of Jewish and Puerto Rican ancestry and worked as a defense attorney at a firm in Rochester.

"I do. 6:45 at the bar, dinner reservations at 7:30."

"You got it. I'm looking forward to spending time with them."

"Me too, I always enjoy their company."

"Ed, I've been so busy I forgot to tell you that Andy Spurling called a couple days ago and asked if I could stop by to see him.

"They're expanding one of the dining rooms at the restaurant and he said he and his crew discovered something in a previously undetected basement he wants to show me, but he wouldn't say what it is, just that it's a surprise. I told him we'd be there on Friday night."

Annie took a sip of tea. "I'm curious, but I'm not going to dwell on it. I have a lot on my plate this week, I'll find out soon enough. Listen, I need to get moving. I'm going to make the sandwiches and then get ready for work."

CHAPTER 3

Within a couple hours, the weather changed and the wind picked up. Waves churned in an angry sea; dark clouds obscured the sun, portending rain. As much as Ed and Annie had looked forward to their outing, they decided to reschedule for another day when, as quickly as it started, the wind died down, the storm clouds dispersed, waves rippled gently onto the shore, and a butter-yellow sun emerged, bright and warm.

Just before noon, Ed filled Gretchen's water bowl, gave her a couple treats, and turned on the TV in the den to a children's program on PBS. Promising her they'd be back, the couple drove to the marina where they boarded their pontoon and headed toward Chimney Bluffs. They chugged along, a regatta of sailboats, colorful sails unfurled, gliding about in the distance. A fishing boat heading out farther into the lake tooted its horn, its skipper waving as he motored by. Gulls shrieked overhead and dive-bombed for tiny fish in the clear water.

Then they heard sirens. A first responders' boat sped by, leaving in its wake a rainbow spray and high waves that slapped against the pontoon, rocking it like a cradle. A few minutes later, now in calmer seas, they anchored several yards off the beach and had begun to unload the picnic gear when they noticed the responders' boat nearby.

"Maybe we should go somewhere else," Annie suggested.

"No, let's keep with the plan. Probably an accident. Hopefully it's nothing serious, although we probably should wait to unpack the boat until we know for sure."

She sighed. "There are so many water-related accidents this time of year, Ed, and it's almost always carelessness that causes them. Wonder what happened this time."

Ed shrugged "Could be anything, Annie, a hiker who wasn't paying attention, walked too close to the edge and fell off the cliff, or someone who ignored the no-swimming signs and got caught in an undertow."

Curious, they waded toward the group. Mike Garfield, the medical examiner, was kneeling beside a body that lay next to an overturned bright yellow kayak near some scrub and tall grasses. Two EMTs, carrying a stretcher, stood next to him talking quietly with tall, handsome Lighthouse Cove police detective Brad Washington, whose dark aviator sunglasses hid his clear, green eyes.

Annie said, "Uh oh, that can't be good."

The medical examiner looked up when he heard the couple talking and motioned for them to approach. The victim, a man about 5'10" tall with a slender build, was lying on his stomach, his face partially buried in the sand.

His long blond hair was tied back into a ponytail. He wore brown leather deck shoes, camo-green and black swim trunks, and a black tee shirt. A few yards behind him, a young woman held the hand of a small girl, who was crying.

Mike said, "She and her daughter were collecting beach stones when she noticed him. He seemed to be sleeping, but something bothered her about the position of his body. She walked over to him to ask if he was okay. When he didn't respond, she bent down to check if he was breathing. When she realized he wasn't, she called 911. Fortunately, there's cell phone service here."

"She doesn't know the victim. I'm going let her and her daughter go; I think they're both in shock." Brad walked over to the woman and started speaking with her.

Shortly after, the detective escorted the mother and child to the parking lot at the top of the bluffs. Mike gently turned the body over.

CHAPTER 4

Annie gasped. "Oh my, I know him."

Mike stared at her. "You do?"

"Yes, his name is Noah Pierce; he's a reporter for the *Rochester Daily News*. He interviewed me before the grand opening of Macyville last summer."

Macyville, a settlement where abolitionists and free people of color had resided from 1813 until the 1920s, had been abandoned and fallen into disrepair before the Great Depression. After receiving a grant from the National Trust for Preservation, the historical society had restored and turned it into a living history museum.

She said, "He wrote an article about the settlement. AP carried it. It created a lot of interest that resulted in a huge number of visitors from all over the United States and Canada.

"Then, several weeks ago he showed up at the museum one morning and asked if I had time to meet with him. I didn't have anything on my schedule until after lunch, so we went into my office and talked.

"He wanted to know if we had any information in our archives about a mysterious boat fire that occurred on the lake a few miles offshore from here during Prohibition. One of his ancestors, a Canadian rumrunner, died in that fire, but he couldn't find anything about it in Canada.

"I'm aware of the fire, but there's nothing at the museum about it, either. Coincidentally, I've just started making notes for next year's exhibit, *Prohibition and Rumrunning on the Lake.* I told him I planned to start my research this fall and offered to share whatever I learned with him.

"He didn't want to wait that long but wasn't sure where to begin. I suggested he visit our library and speak with our head librarian, Holly Corcoran. We made a deal that if he found anything I could use for our exhibit he'd share it with me, and I'd list him in our promotional materials as a contributor."

"Do you know if he was making progress?" Brad asked.

"Yes. He texted me a week ago."

She pulled her phone out of her pocket and said, "Good. I kept it. '*Making great progress. Library's archives contain digitized newspaper articles I can use, found other sources, too. Talk soon.*' He added a smiling emoji."

She paused. "I wonder if his being here at Chimney Bluffs had something to do with that project."

"I wouldn't read anything into it just yet," Mike cautioned. "The most likely explanation is that he kayaked here early this morning, had an accident and drowned."

Removing his sunglasses, Brad asked Annie, "Do you happen to know anything about his personal life?"

"I do. After he finished interviewing me about Macyville, and before he left to go back to Rochester, I gave him cookies and iced tea and we chatted for several minutes. His parents live in Gananoque, Ontario, where he grew up, but he has dual citizenship. His mother was born in the states.

"He received bachelor's and master's degrees in journalism from the Newhouse School at Syracuse University. He's single and lives in the city in the Neighborhood of the Arts. I think he said he rents an apartment on Oxford Street."

"Thanks. That helps. I'm going to need to notify his parents as soon as possible," the detective said.

"They'll be devastated," Annie replied. "I got the sense from him that they're a very close family."

Mike held up his hand and said, "People. I'd like to examine his body and would appreciate some quiet. Perhaps you could continue this conversation later?"

Several minutes later he looked up and said, "As I thought, this appears to be a simple drowning. There are some strong undercurrents here. It's likely the kayak overturned and when he went into the water his body hit some rocks which resulted in the bruises and that gash on the back of his head. Although with no witnesses to attest to what happened to him, I'm legally required to conduct a post-mortem."

"He couldn't have possibly kayaked here all the way from Rochester, Mike; it would have taken hours," Ed observed.

"Good point, and in that case his car should be parked in the visitors' lot. I'll check to see if a driver's license and keys are in one of his pockets," Brad responded.

The brown-skinned detective, who was wearing a sage green safari shirt and tan khakis, retrieved a pair of nitrile gloves from a back pocket and a few seconds later removed a small waterproof pouch from the victim's swim trunks. It contained a wallet, driver's license, credit and debit cards, a press pass; and as he hoped, a house key and one for a Honda Civic.

"What about a cell phone?" Ed asked.

"Nope. I'm assuming he left it in his car. If not, then my best guess is it's somewhere at the bottom of the lake," Brad responded.

"Ladies and gents, I'd like to stay and chat but time's a' wasting. I need to get this young man's body to the morgue."

Brad responded that he was going to stay and check the parking lot for the car. If it was there, he'd call a tow truck company to transport it with the kayak to the police station. He assumed the victim's parents would want them, or should the post-mortem reveal his death the result of foul play, for the forensic techs to begin a criminal investigation.

He asked Ed and Annie if they could stick around. If he found the car, he'd hitch a ride to the station with the tow truck driver; if not, he'd need transportation to Lighthouse Cove with the kayak.

"I expect this is not how you planned your day, and if you'd rather not stay I can call Mia to pick me up; she's on patrol today," he said.

Annie was pale and edgy and said she wanted to go home but urged Ed to stay and help Brad. Mike said if she wasn't too uncomfortable with the victim's body being onboard, she could ride with him and the EMTs to the morgue and someone from his office would drive her home from there.

CHAPTER 5

As they began climbing the steep, winding path that led from the beach to the picnic area and parking lot, Brad hesitated. "Wait a minute, Ed. I want to call the DMV and get Pierce's license plate number. Civics are popular; there could be more than one up there."

The investigators located two, but neither belonged to the victim. "Ed, I agree with you that it's highly unlikely our victim kayaked all the way from Rochester, but then how did he get here?"

"I'm guessing, of course, but one possibility is that he was staying with a friend who lives nearby, or another is that someone drove him here, dropped him off and planned on picking him up later today. In either case I expect you'll receive a call reporting that he's missing." Ed responded.

The two men spoke with picnickers and a few hikers who had come off the trail. No one knew Noah or had seen anything odd or suspicious.

They walked back down the path to the beach, lifted the kayak and started carrying it to the pontoon when someone yelled, "Excuse me, what are you doing with my kayak? Put it down now, or I'll call the cops."

They turned to see a young man who appeared to be in his twenties running toward them. Brad pulled his badge out of a shirt pocket.

"I'm with the Lighthouse Cove police department. This is yours?"

"It is. My name is Tim Miller. My parents own a cottage over there on Crescent Beach." He pointed to a nearby island.

"I'm visiting them this week from Pittsburgh. I paddled here early this morning to meet some friends from Fulton, which is where I grew up. We cooked breakfast on one of the grills in the park and spent the rest of the morning hiking the bluff. I left the kayak on the beach, it's too awkward to carry up that path without help. I've done it before and have never had a problem."

Brad asked for the young man's ID and explained that they'd found a dead body next to the kayak and believed it belonged to the victim. He pulled a driver's license out of his pocket and handed it to the detective.

"Sorry for the confusion, Mr. Miller." Brad handed the ID back to him.

"I'm sorry someone died, but I assure you that kayak is mine."

"I believe you. What time did you get here?"

"About 7:00."

"Was there anyone else on the beach?"

"Nope."

"All right, then. You're free to go. Have a good day."

They watched as he walked away with the kayak; then waded into the water to the pontoon.

"Brad, you should call Mike and let him know about the kayak."

The detective and medical examiner spoke for several minutes. After the conversation ended, he turned to Ed and said,

"Now that we know our victim didn't have an accident with the kayak, '*what further inferences may we draw?*'"

Ed laughed. "What? Where did that come from?"

Brad grinned. "Sir Arthur Conan Doyle. When I was a kid I got hooked on reading mysteries, especially Sherlock Holmes. *The Hound of the Baskervilles* was one of my favorites. I can also quote from Agatha Christie, Raymond Chandler, Dashiell Hammett."

"Brad, you never cease to amaze me. *What we may infer is that perhaps a murderous villain is afoot.*"

"Shakespeare?"

"No, Ed DeCleryk."

Brad rolled his eyes.

CHAPTER 6

The two men chatted amiably as Ed headed back to Lighthouse Cove. The lake was calm, and they were making good time. As they neared the channel that led into Silver Bay he asked Brad about Carrie Ramos, the police chief. "I haven't seen her for a while, how's she doing?"

"She's doing great. She and Matt are spending the week in Montreal and Quebec; her parents are watching Natalya and Arturo. They'll be back on Saturday afternoon "

"Are you in charge until she returns?"

"I am." He grinned. "She was going to announce it next week; she'll be fine with my telling you now. She promoted me to deputy chief just before they left for vacation. I'll be wearing two hats until Mia passes her detective exam; after that, she'll replace me as detective, and we'll hire a new patrol person. You know how responsible Carrie is; with my promotion she'll be able to take vacation time without feeling guilty."

"You're perfect for the job, Brad, and expanding the police department makes sense, especially with the influx of newcomers to our growing community."

"Carrie and I discussed it and if you're interested, we'd still like you to work with us as a criminal consultant. We expect there will be times like this when we'll need to draw upon your experience and expertise."

Ed smiled. "I am. I've been thinking about retiring, but truth be told I'm not quite ready yet and Annie announced this morning that she plans to continue working for several more years."

A few minutes later Ed pulled into the public dock at the village municipal beach. The investigators decided to check for Noah's car in the parking lot, wondering if he may have met someone there who transported him to Chimney Bluffs, but again, they struck out. The mystery deepened.

Ed dropped the detective off at the dock behind the police station, then sailed to the marina, guided the pontoon into its slip and made a couple trips back and forth to his SUV with the picnic gear. When he arrived home, Annie and her friend, Eve Beauvoir, were sitting on Adirondack chairs facing the water, sipping glasses of lemonade. Eve stood and hugged Ed. He bent down to kiss his wife.

"I realized I didn't want to be alone until you got back, so I called Eve to keep me company. It's so nice that she lives two blocks away now; it would have been an imposition to ask her before she and Henri moved here from White Pelican Island. Did you find Noah's car?"

"No, and the kayak wasn't his, either. It belonged to a young man who had paddled to Chimney Bluffs earlier this morning from Crescent Beach to meet some friends."

Eve said, "Annie, now that Ed's home, I'm going to go home. Henri's sister and brother-in-law will be arriving later this afternoon from Quebec and staying with us for several days. I want to get dinner started."

"Oh my, Eve. Why didn't you say something? If I had realized you were expecting company I never would have called."

"Annie, it's no problem. I'm pleased you felt comfortable asking for my support, and I know you'd do the same for me."

With tears in her eyes, Annie stood and hugged her friend. "Thank you."

The DeCleryks walked Eve to her car, unloaded the SUV and since neither of them was hungry, placed the sandwiches, tarts and beverages from the picnic cooler in the refrigerator to eat later for dinner. Annie went to the living room to read a book; Ed to his study to listen to music. Two hours later, his phone rang.

CHAPTER 7

"Ed, it's Brad. Mike called; he's finished with the post-mortem and while he can't conclusively prove Pierce was murdered, he is ruling his death as suspicious. The official cause is drowning, but before entering the water he was hit by a hard object that resulted in a concussion and bruises on his body that don't appear to have been caused by rocks."

"Someone assaulted him and then pushed him into the water?"

"That's Mike's opinion, and most likely from a boat. But it will be up to us to find out exactly what happened to him. Mike pulled what he believes to be slivers of a type of fiberglass that's commonly used in boat building from a wound in his head and marine carpet fibers that were embedded the soles of his shoes."

"He's sending everything to the crime lab for analysis but cautioned that they probably won't be successful in identifying any DNA other than Pierce's; it tends to disintegrate when a body has been submerged in water for a while."

"Have you contacted Carrie?"

"I texted her. There's nothing she can do until she gets back, but she thanked me for keeping her in the loop and asked me to say hello to you. If you're available, she'd like you to work the case with me."

"I am. Did Mike indicate time of death?"

"He's guestimating between 7:30 and 9:00 this morning, but he may have been in the water for several hours before his body washed up onto the beach."

"Any drugs or alcohol in his system?"

"No. No health issues, either."

"Have you had time to do a background check?"

"Squeaky clean. Not even a parking ticket. And by the way, I had a hunch about his car. I called the Rochester police; they located it in the tenants' lot behind his building, so we still don't know how he got to Chimney Bluffs. I'll be meeting forensic techs and a couple of Rochester city detectives at his apartment sometime tomorrow to begin our investigation."

Changing the subject, Ed said, "How about if I call the editor of the *Rochester Daily News* to schedule an interview? I'm wondering if our victim was working on an assignment that put him in danger. "

"Good idea. Hopefully she'll be available to speak with you as soon as possible."

"Did you track down his parents?"

"I did. Annie was correct, they live in Gananoque. I didn't feel comfortable notifying them over the phone, but it would have taken me three hours to drive there. I called their police chief who went to their house and spoke with them. He said they are heartbroken, as you would expect. They're on their way here now. I located a room for them at the Wisteria Inn; fortunately, there was a last-minute cancellation. Every other place was booked solid."

"What time are they meeting with Mike?"

"8:00 tomorrow morning. They'll take their son's personal effects back to Canada with them; a funeral parlor in Gananoque will transport his body."

"Are you planning to interview them after they're finished speaking with Mike?"

"Yes, at 9:00 in my office. Are you available?"

"I am."

"Brad, have you taken any breaks today? Have you eaten?"

"I had breakfast, but nothing since then, and no, I've not taken any breaks. I wanted to get a head start on the investigation."

"You must be exhausted. Go home, be with your wife, there's nothing more you can do this evening."

"I know. I'm leaving as soon as you and I are finished talking."

Annie had walked out of the room to give Ed privacy. He found her in the living room reading a magazine and summarized the conversation.

"Annie, for some reason I'm having a déjà vu moment about this case."

"Could it be similar to one you've investigated in the past?"

"No. I just can't fathom what's making me feel so unsettled."

"Stop thinking about it; it'll come to you."

The couple spent the rest of the evening watching comedy shows on TV. That night neither of them slept well, disturbed by a series of unsettling nightmares.

CHAPTER 8

At 8:45 the next morning, carrying two coffees and freshly baked blueberry muffins from Bistro Louise, Ed entered the police station, walked down the hall and into Brad's office. The young detective was sitting at his desk pounding away at his keyboard. He looked up.

"Hi, Ed. Give me a minute, I'm just about finished writing notes for our meeting with Pierce's parents."

A couple minutes later Ed handed him a coffee and muffin. "I figured you probably were here at the crack of dawn."

"I woke up at 3:30 this morning and couldn't fall back asleep so I decided to get up and come into the office. I got here about 5:00."

"Something troubling you about this case?"

"Sort of. Mike didn't entirely rule out that Pierce's death was an accident. I felt like I owed it to his parents to at least explore that possibility. As tragic as it is, it still would be easier for them to accept.

"I wondered if perhaps instead of being on someone else's boat, he rented one from a marina, planning to sail to Chimney Bluffs to see if he could find the approximate location on the lake where his ancestor died in that fire.

"Remember, the lake was choppy yesterday morning, there was a storm brewing, and if he had no experience sailing in rough waters, he could have had a mishap. And that might explain his missing phone. If he tried calling 911 and the boat got hit by a wave, he could have dropped it into the lake and then after that became injured, fell into the water and drowned."

"Good thinking, Brad."

"Anyway, before I left for home last night, I called Mike and asked that he send a death certificate to Noah's bank before he closed shop for the day. I wanted to check debit and credit card transactions to see if there were any charges on either of them from local marinas. After that I called the bank and spoke with the manager. She said once they received the certificate they'd fax me the information, probably sometime this morning.

"Before I went to bed last night I read yesterday's police logs to see if any of the marinas had reported a missing or stolen boat, but there were none. Then I thought if he rented a boat for 24 hours, a report might not have been filed yet."

"But if he rented a boat, Brad, how would he have gotten to the marina?"

"I thought about that, too, and wondered if Noah scheduled a ride with a rideshare company. I emailed all of them when I got here; last time I looked there were no responses. Let me check again."

He logged into his computer and scrolled through his emails. "They've all responded. Unfortunately, I didn't get the answer I wanted; there were no pick-ups at his address at any time yesterday."

Just then Barb Snowden, the police department receptionist, rapped on his door and entered. "I think this is the fax you've been waiting for."

She handed it to him, and he glanced at it. "No credit charges at marinas, either. I completely struck out."

"What you did was good detecting, Brad. You covered all bases. I think it's probably now safe to assume he was injured and subsequently drowned while on the boat of the person who killed him."

"I agree, but it's going to be a challenge to find out who that person is."

"We'll figure it out. Changing the subject, how would you like to handle the interview with Pierce's parents? Do you want me there as an observer or participant?"

"Participant. I could use your help. I'm tired and feeling a bit overwhelmed."

"Piece of advice?"

"Sure."

"Set a limit for how many hours you're going to work each day and after that let it go.

"Annie and I are solid; she's always been supportive and patient, but at times when we were younger my obsession with work and solving murder cases put a strain on our relationship."

Instead of responding, Brad bit off a piece of muffin, and rolled his eyes. "Baked from scratch, still warm, blueberry, what more could a guy ask for? Thank you. This is delicious."

Seconds later he said, "I'm not ignoring you, Ed. I appreciate your concern, and you're right. Felicia has also advised me to set boundaries. As the morning news anchor of a major TV network, my wife certainly understands pressure. She's awake before dawn five days a week, but when she's finished for the day, she seems to be able to leave work behind. I'll try to find a way to balance things out."

CHAPTER 9

Barb escorted Julie and Sam Pierce to Brad's office promptly at 9:00 a.m. where he greeted them and introduced Ed. In their early 50s, the couple looked older, their bodies sagged, their eyes were red-rimmed; they were pale and listless. They said the accommodations at the inn were comfortable; still, they hadn't slept a wink the night before.

They sat on leather swivel chairs at a round oak table in one corner, sunlight streaming though tall windows with a view of the bay. Despite the brightness, the weight of their grief was palpable and cast a dark shadow upon the room.

An insulated thermos filled with coffee had been placed on a credenza along one wall, a tray next to it with mugs, a bowl of sugar, and a small pitcher of cream.

Another thermos contained hot water, and beside it on another tray, an assortment of teas and a bowl filled with lemon slices. Julie accepted a cup of tea; Sam declined a beverage.

Blond like her son, Julie wore cropped wide-legged white linen slacks, a pale blue linen short-sleeved top and white leather sandals. She'd tossed a white cotton sweater over her shoulders and nervously plucked at one of the sleeves. Her husband, dressed in a navy golf shirt, khaki slacks and brown loafers without socks, ran his hands through his short brown hair, then rubbed them together as though trying to stay warm.

"I'm truly sorry for your loss," Brad began. "I can't begin to imagine how painful this is for you."

Julie started to cry. Her husband leaned toward her and put his arm around her shoulders. She took a deep, shaky breath. "I don't think we could survive this without the support of our family and close friends.

"Our daughter, Hannah, and her husband, Josh, live in Toronto but wanted to be with us today, we convinced them to stay where they are. Our granddaughter, Olivia, is only two months old; the trip would have been difficult. Now she'll never get to know her kind and loving uncle, and whatever plans Noah had for his life are destroyed."

She started crying again.

Ed said, "At some point, we'll want to speak with Hannah; not today of course, but soon. Sometime siblings confide in each other without telling their parents; she may have information that will help with our investigation."

"I'll give you her phone number before we leave," Julie responded, wiping her eyes.

Brad asked "Are you sure you're okay speaking with us this morning? We can reschedule if you aren't up to it."

"There's never going to be a perfect time, we might as well get this over with so we can take our son back to Gananoque," Sam responded. "I feel like I'm living in a nightmare, and I'm never going to wake up. You're certain our son's death wasn't an accident?"

"It's not looking that way. The evidence is pointing to foul play." Brad said.

"I guess I was grasping at straws."

"Completely understandable, what happened to Noah is a parent's nightmare. Later this morning I'll be joining a team of investigators from Rochester to see if we can find any evidence in his apartment or car that can help us solve the crime."

He continued. "At some point we'll be able to release all his personal effects to you, but it might not be for several days."

"We understand," Sam said.

Julie sighed and shook her head. "I don't."

"Is that a problem?" Brad asked.

"Not for most of his things. He just renewed his lease, so we have plenty of time to empty his apartment, and honestly, I don't think either of us has the energy to do it right now. But there is something I'd like back before then, if possible," Julie responded.

"Before my parents married, my dad served in Vietnam and was awarded bronze and silver stars. He passed away a few years ago. Hannah received the bronze and Noah, the silver. A jeweler made it into a pendant that he wore on a silver chain around his neck.

"He hardly ever took it off except to bathe, sleep or participate in an activity that might have damaged it. It's not worth much monetarily, but there's a lot of sentimental value to it. I'm not concerned about anyone stealing it, but I am concerned about leaving it in his apartment until we get back to clean it out. I wouldn't want anyone to accidentally discard it." She started crying again.

The detective took a sip of coffee. "He was wearing swim trunks when we found him, it's probably still there. Any idea where he kept it?"

Julie answered, "He stored it in a carved rosewood box lined with black velvet. It should be on top of his dresser or in a drawer."

Brad thought for a moment. "What time are you leaving to go back to Gananoque today?"

"Not until later this afternoon after the funeral home comes to pick up Noah's body. We have to check out of the inn by 11:00, but the innkeepers said we were welcome to use the public spaces until then. Why?"

"I'll call you before I leave here for Rochester later this morning; you can follow me, and I'll let you into Noah's apartment. If the medal's there we'll dust it for prints and then you can take it along with you."

"That's wonderful. Thank you."

Ed changed the subject, "My wife, Annie, runs our local historical society and museum and mentioned that Noah visited her not too long ago. He was planning on doing research about one of your ancestors who died in a mysterious boat fire on the lake near Chimney Bluffs during Prohibition and asked if the museum had information about it.

"Unfortunately, she couldn't help him but suggested he visit our local library. He promised to share any information he found with her and texted about a week ago saying he was making progress. Did he mention anything to you about it?"

Sam said, "He did and we got the same message. The ancestor was one of my great-grandfathers, a rumrunner. He was barely in his twenties and left a young wife and newborn son. He's buried along with the rest of our family in an old cemetery adjacent to our church. The case went cold in Canada, which is why he thought he'd see if he could find anything about it in Lighthouse Cove. We were eager to learn what he discovered."

"I'm assuming he owned a laptop. Do you know if he used it or one from work for his research?"

"His own. He wasn't permitted to use his work computer for personal projects," Sam responded.

"Do you think he was killed because of something to do with his research?" Julie asked.

"It's early days. That Noah's body was washed up on the beach at Chimney Bluffs may be for a completely different reason, perhaps a newspaper assignment or something personal. I promise, we'll do everything we can to find his killer and make sure that person is put away for life," Brad answered.

CHAPTER 10

"We'd like to speak with his friends. Can you help us?" Brad asked.

Julie said, "Yes. He kept in touch with several from high school and college. A few of his college friends joined him when he visited us a couple weekends ago. Most of them remained in Syracuse after they graduated, so it was an easy drive."

"I can provide you with their names, but I don't have phone numbers or addresses. That information should be in his cell phone."

"We're still looking for his phone; it may have fallen into the water or been destroyed by the person who did this to him. If we can't locate it we'll send a death certificate to the phone company so we can retrieve his records, but it could take a few days," Brad responded.

"Did he seem disturbed about anything during that visit? How was his mood?" Ed asked.

"He was fine. Happy and easygoing as usual. The weather was magnificent. They took our pontoon out on Saturday morning; we live near the St. Lawrence River, and the rest of the weekend they hung out, played cards, drank beer, watched sports on TV; the typical way young men spend a weekend."

Julie requested paper and a pen; a few minutes later she handed the paper to Brad. "These are his friends' names and our daughter's contact information. Noah was also friendly with two young reporters at the newspaper."

"Thanks for that information. I'm planning to call his editor today to schedule an interview and at the same time will ask to speak with them," Ed responded.

"Was he dating anyone?" Brad asked.

"Yes, but he never mentioned her name. Our sense was it was never serious, the last time we spoke he said he'd ended it."

"What about when he was in college?"

Julie nodded. "Her name is Stacy Morgan. They met when they were sophomores and were together until they received their master's degrees at Newhouse. When they graduated she wanted to get married.

"Noah had been offered a job writing for the *Rochester Daily News*. Stacy pressured him not to take it. She'd been hired as an editor for a regional magazine, *On the Spot in Syracuse,* and pleaded with him to stay there and find a job. He refused; he wanted to work at the paper in Rochester.

"He suggested they continue seeing each other on weekends; it's only an hour and a half trip between the two cities, and then after a year if they were still together they could talk about next steps. That wasn't acceptable. Instead, she gave him an ultimatum: find a job in Syracuse and commit to getting married within the year or the relationship was over.

"It took strength and he agonized about it, but he didn't like being threatened and broke up with her. She was shocked and said she hadn't really meant what she'd said, but he realized he didn't want to be with someone who was so controlling and manipulative. We supported him; he'd made the right decision. We were never overly fond of her."

Sam said, "Stacy called her father and informed him that Noah had broken up with her but didn't tell him why. Jim called our son and berated him for the way he'd handled the breakup and said that Stacy was completely blindsided.

"Noah quickly set the record straight. Jim called him a liar, hung up on him, but called a couple days later and apologized. When he confronted Stacy she confessed that what Noah had told him was true.

"We're not aware of any contact between them after that, and I can't imagine that either of them would carry a grudge and want to harm our son, but Noah is a grown man and didn't tell us everything."

Ed asked, "How well did you know Jim? Did he ever give you reason to believe he could be violent? "

Sam responded, "I don't think so, but we only spent time with him at college functions and during some holidays. He was always pleasant. Stacy is an only child; he was awarded full custody after he and her mother divorced and she relocated to the West Coast. We both thought he was overly protective of her and a little too indulgent."

Brad stood up, walked over to the credenza and brought the water and tea bags to the table and when she nodded, poured Julie another cup. "Do you have their phone numbers? Even if neither had anything to do with Noah's death, we'd like to speak with them."

"No, but unless he's changed jobs, Jim is head of security at the power plant near Rochester," Julie responded.

Sam said Stacy was probably still working for the magazine. If not, her father could provide them with her contact information.

CHAPTER 11

"When was the last time you spoke with Noah?" Ed asked.

"Several days ago," Sam replied. "We wanted to spend time with our new grandbaby and drove to Toronto this past weekend. We asked him if he wanted to join us; he declined. He said he had other plans."

"When did you return to Gananoque?"

"Late Sunday afternoon."

"Anything unusual happen after you got back?"

"Nothing. We did what we usually do when we return from a trip and the weather is nice. We took our boat out and stopped for dinner at a restaurant on the river and then came home and watched TV for the rest of the evening."

"What about yesterday, before your police chief contacted you? Did you receive any strange phone calls?"

"No," Sam said. "We work from home; we both had virtual staff meetings yesterday morning. After that we met some friends for lunch; a couple hours later our police chief paid us a visit. I never in a million years could have predicted that the reason was to tell us about Noah." He wiped his eyes.

Ed asked, "I can't being to imagine how shattered you must have been. Have you scheduled the funeral?"

Sam responded, "We have; mid-morning a week from this Saturday at the church where our family worships.

"It seems like a long time to wait, but the pastor has other commitments before then. We want her to officiate; she's a close family friend. Some relatives who live in western Canada and England will also need time to arrange for travel to Gananoque."

Ed asked the Pierces if he and Annie could attend the funeral, not only to pay their respects but also for him to speak with their family and friends, should any of them be able to provide information that could help with the investigation.

The couple was silent for a moment; then Julie said, "Mr. DeCleryk, burying Noah will be more difficult for us than you can possibly imagine, but what is even harder is not knowing why he died and who killed him. Certainly, you are welcome attend the funeral."

The interview ended; Brad promised he'd call them when he was ready to leave for Rochester, and the Pierce's went back to the bed and breakfast.

Ed said, "I'm impressed with how well you handled the interview, Brad. You were thorough, but also very kind."

"Thanks; it was a joint effort. I've learned a lot from you since we started working together."

He paused. "I believed them when they told us about their weekend and how they spent their day yesterday, but to officially rule them out I need to find a way to confirm their alibi. I'm not sure how to do it. I don't want to cause more stress for them by insinuating that they may have been involved in their son's death. In my heart I know they're innocent. They have more than enough to deal with right now."

"Call the Gananoque police chief," Ed suggested. "He'll be discreet and should be able to verify their whereabouts during the past several days."

"That makes sense. I'll call him in a few minutes."

Ed responded, "And I'll call the newspaper editor and try to schedule time with her for this afternoon. One of us should also contact Stacy Morgan and her father. Can you ask Barb to get their phone numbers?"

"Sure thing. Give me a minute; I'll be right back." Brad walked down the hall to the reception area. While he was gone, Ed called Carol Smalley, the newspaper editor, and arranged to meet with her and the two young reporters as soon as he could get to Rochester.

Brad reported that Barb would text them with Jim and Stacy Morgan's contact information as soon as she located it, which, because she was so efficient, occurred minutes later.

CHAPTER 12

A hot sun burned brightly in a cloudless sky as Ed drove the scenic route along Lake Ontario to Rochester.

To the north, sparkling diamonds of light bounced off the water while foaming white waves gently rolled onto the beach. A smattering of fishing boats clustered in groups a half mile offshore, where an abundance of steelhead, salmon and trout had been spotted.

He passed through the quaint, historic hamlet of Pultneyville, admiring charming Federal-style homes, imposing Victorians and a scenic harbor inlet carved into the land.

Before the road ended at a channel where boats sailed into the lake from Irondequoit Bay, Ed turned left toward the highway and then drove west across the bay bridge, high above the water, with vistas reminiscent of coastal Cornwall paintings: boats drifting about, cottages snugged into cozy coves, and in the distance, the vast, broad expanse of teal-blue water that stretched to the horizon.

Several minutes later he parked his car across the street from the newspaper office and entered the three-story brick building where a security guard directed him to the third floor. He decided he needed the exercise; instead of taking the elevator, he climbed the stairs.

When he reached the landing slightly breathless, he opened a heavy metal door and entered the brightly lit newsroom—a large open space filled with cubicles where reporters were either speaking on their phones or busily pounding away at laptop computers.

In the far corner, a glassed-in office with the editor's name engraved on a brass plaque on the door faced the newsroom. He walked toward it, and a tall, lean woman with short blond hair streaked with gray, and hazel eyes behind large, round, black-framed reading glasses, emerged and introduced herself.

She wore a light denim shirtwaist dress, black flats, small, gold hoop earrings, and a thick gold wedding band. Ed followed her into the office. They sat across from one another at her desk. She offered him coffee; he declined.

"Your last name is familiar, Mr. DeCleryk. How do I know it?"

"My wife runs the historical society and museum in Lighthouse Cove. Noah interviewed her about Macyville, a settlement established by abolitionists and free people of color before and during the Civil War. It was recently restored as a living history museum."

"Of course. I remember now. AP picked it up. My husband and I toured the property shortly after the article was published. What a treasure."

"It is. My wife appreciated the publicity. It's resulted in far more visitors than she anticipated. Now, what can you tell me about Noah?"

"He was a good writer, and also a young man of incredible character, wise beyond his years. He died way too young, and I can't begin to fathom why anyone would want to harm him."

Ed asked when she'd seen him last; she said it had been on Friday afternoon. He mentioned that he probably wouldn't be back in the office until Monday afternoon, he had personal business to attend to in the morning.

"Of course, he never returned. I am horrified, Ed, about what happened to him."

"Was that typical of him to take personal time during the week?"

"No, but our reporters sometimes work evenings and weekends. I have no problem with their occasionally taking a few hours off for personal reasons."

"I'm assuming you provided him with a laptop; I noticed that each of your reporters had one at their desks. Would he have taken it when he left for the weekend? His parents thought he was only permitted to use it for work."

"They're correct. It should be here and locked away in his desk. I have a master key."

Ed followed her to Noah's desk. She opened the top drawer.

"Good, it's here."

"May I borrow it for a few days? There may be information in it that can help us figure out what happened to him."

"If I lend it to you, you'll need to return it in 48 hours. Instead, how about if I copy all his files onto a USB drive?"

"Even better. Thanks."

CHAPTER 13

"What can you tell me about his recent assignments?" Ed asked. "Was there anything he was working on that could have put him in danger?"

"Not at all. He was writing profiles on local community leaders; we've started featuring one a week in our Sunday paper."

She continued, "Noah was creative, and even though this was a straightforward assignment he decided to interview family members, mainly parents and grandparents, curious about how they may have influenced his subjects' career decisions. He completed half the interviews; I believe he'd scheduled most of the remaining ones."

"Any problems? Anyone seem hostile or refuse to be interviewed?"

"Not that he said, although he was unable to schedule an interview with Robert Lessley, the head of our chamber of commerce. Noah called him several times, and each time he claimed he was too busy and had too much on his plate to meet with him.

"As a result, he won't be part of the series, which is unfortunate. He's successfully brought a multitude of businesses to the Rochester area, and I think readers would enjoy learning more about him, but it is what it is."

"What's going to happen now?"

"We'll posthumously publish the articles he completed with his by-line; I'll assign another reporter to finish the assignment."

"I'd like to speak with everyone on that list."

"Their names and contact information should be in his computer files."

"Any complaints about Noah?"

"None, but lots of praise. He was easy to work with and always polite and professional."

"What else did he write?"

"He wrote general news articles and feature stories. He expressed interest in becoming an investigative reporter, and I think he would have made a good one. For starters I assigned him to see what he could dig up about the commercial fishing industry on the US side of Lake Ontario. It's legal in Canada, but not here.

"The Fish and Game Commission and Coast Guard have informed us that the industry is growing. They believe charter boat captains are providing freshly caught lake fish to local restaurants. Supposedly, it's a lucrative business."

"I didn't know that. I always assumed when we order lake fish that the restaurants purchase their fish from Canada. Had he started yet?"

"I suggested he complete the Sunday series first, but he was eager to begin the project. I gave him the go-ahead to as long as it didn't affect his other work."

"Then those notes should be in his computer."

"Possibly."

Ed said, "Did he ever mention a boat fire that occurred on Lake Ontario during Prohibition? One of his ancestors was killed, but he couldn't find any information about it in Canada and was hoping that our historical society might be a resource. He spoke with my wife who directed him to our community library."

"Yes, just in passing. It sounded interesting to me; our readers enjoy learning about local history. I said to let me know what he found; I might ask him to write a feature story. The last thing I heard is that he was making progress, but there wouldn't be anything about it in this computer since it wasn't an official work assignment."

"Our deputy chief, Brad Washington, and a team of investigators from the city are searching Noah's car and apartment this morning. If his laptop's there, it should contain a file with that information. I'll keep you posted."

"Thank you."

"You said you were in the office yesterday. What time did you arrive?"

"I've been waiting for you to ask. I got in early, around 7:15. I often come in on weekends, at least for a couple of hours, but I decided to take Sunday off; our children and grandchildren came over for a barbecue. We have cameras at the entrance to the building with time stamps; I can give you a copy."

"That's not necessary. I believe you, but thanks for offering."

She paused. "Ed, where do you go from here?"

"There are multiple scattered puzzle pieces; it's going to take time to put them together. If you don't mind, before I meet with your reporters I'd like to take a couple minutes to check in with Brad.

"Of course not. Ajani and Melissa are waiting for you in the conference room. I'll take you to them when you're finished."

CHAPTER 14

Ed texted Brad: *"How's it going?"* A few seconds later, his phone rang.

"I figured it would be easier to call than text you, Ed. We found the medal; it was in the top drawer of Noah's dresser. His parents were delighted and thanked me profusely for letting them take it back to Canada with them. We did dust it for prints, but I expect the only ones we'll find will be Noah's.

"His laptop is missing. We couldn't locate a USB or external hard drive, which leads us to believe that he backed everything up to the Cloud, but without a username and password there's no way to access it.

"I expect he saved that information, along with other usernames and passwords, to a file on his computer; most people do. I was hoping, as a safeguard in case something happened to his computer, that he'd also stored a printed copy somewhere.

"We've checked everywhere; nothing. I guess it's possible if there weren't many, he could have committed them to memory. The techs found fingerprints, hair strands and fibers they'll take to the crime lab for analysis.

"We didn't find his cell phone, and the phone company won't release a record of his transactions until they receive the death certificate. They should have it by now; I'll contact them later and request that they email a copy to me.

"Are you still at the newspaper office?"

"I am. I just finished interviewing the editor and will be speaking with the two young reporters in a couple minutes. How about if we touch base later?"

"I think we'll be here for a while; I'll call you when I get back to Lighthouse Cove."

Carol Smalley was waiting outside her office. She entered when she saw Ed place his phone back in his pocket. "If you're ready, I'll take you to meet Ajani and Melissa."

"Before we go, I hope you don't mind my asking: was there competition among the three of them for choice assignments?"

She shook her head. "Ajani writes arts and entertainment features; Melissa covers sports. They're both very happy where they are, and Noah had no desire to do anything different. The three of them were close friends."

She paused. "Would you happen to have his parents' address and funeral details? I'd like to send a condolence card with flowers and pay my respects, if possible."

"Yes, the funeral will be a week from Saturday. When I get home, I'll email you details and their contact information."

"I appreciate it. We're all horrified about what happened to Noah and very sad about his tragic and untimely death. I hope you are able to apprehend his killer quickly."

CHAPTER 15

The reporters sat at a table holding hands and talking quietly. When Ed entered the room, they stood and introduced themselves.

A young woman, small with a wiry build, short, curly brown hair and brown eyes, sniffed and wiped her eyes with her sleeve, then said, "I'm Melissa Duncan. Carol said you want to speak with us about Noah. I can't believe he's dead. It's just horrible."

A tall, slender, ebony-skinned young man with a five o'clock shadow, short, cropped black hair and large, expressive dark brown eyes with long lashes, shook Ed's hand. "I'm Ajani Amibola, also very sad about Noah."

Ed smiled. "Nigerian?"

Ajani grinned. "Yes. My parents emigrated from Lagos when I was four. They're professors at the University of Rochester. How'd you know?"

Ed grinned back. "In a previous life I was a Navy SEAL; we conducted a rescue mission in Nigeria many years ago. I can't go into details, but I'm adept at languages and recognized your accent."

"Impressive."

"Please sit. I know how distressing this must be for you. I won't take up much of your time, but for starters and to get it out of the way, I must ask about your whereabouts yesterday. This is just routine; you're not in any trouble."

Neither reporter was offended. Both had been in the office; they arrived a little later than Carol. She could vouch for them.

"When was the last time you saw Noah?"

"Friday afternoon," Melissa answered. "My boyfriend, Pete, and I spent the weekend with my parents and siblings at our family's cabin in the Adirondacks. I invited him to join us, but he said he had plans with neighbors who also lived in his building. They were going to Durand-Eastman Park for a picnic on the beach on Saturday, and he thought he might meet up with some college friends in Syracuse on Sunday."

"That's the last time I saw him, too," Ajani responded, "Like Melissa, I had plans with my family for the weekend. I invited him to join me on Saturday. We attended a picnic sponsored by the Nigerian Association of Greater Rochester. I have a beautiful cousin, a grad student at R.I.T., who I thought he might like and wanted to introduce them. He said he was interested but it would have to be another time."

Ed nodded. Julie Pierce had provided the names of his college friends, and the landlord could probably give him the phone numbers of the young tenants.

"Do you know if Noah used social media? I'd like to check if anyone posted threats."

Melissa replied, "I don't think he did anything on Facebook; mostly that's for older folks like you." She blushed. "Sorry, that didn't come out the way I meant it."

Ed grinned. "No offense taken. It's true. Where does your generation post?"

"Mostly on TikTok and Instagram. If he had accounts, I don't know if he used his real name or a fictitious one," Melissa answered.

She looked at Ajani. "Do you?"

"I do. We talked about it. He wasn't the least bit interested in posting on social media unless it was work related. I don't know what name he used, but Carol could probably tell you."

"I'll check with her on my way out," Ed responded, "The two of you obviously spent lots of time with Noah when you weren't working. What can you tell me about his personal life?"

CHAPTER 16

Melissa said the three of them had started at the paper at approximately the same time and quickly became friends. They hung out together after work and occasionally on weekends; sometimes her boyfriend joined them.

Mostly, they went to bars or clubs in the neighborhood or to concerts and sporting events. In the winter they went snowboarding at Brantling, a ski resort located near Lighthouse Cove, or Bristol Mountain, just outside of Canandaigua. Sometimes, when conditions were right, they windsurfed on the lake.

"When I spoke with Noah's parents, they mentioned he'd been dating someone but said he'd never talked much about her and believed the relationship had ended. Did you meet her?"

"Yes. Her name is Belinda Corey," Melissa answered.

Ajani said, "A bunch of us went to a bar one Saturday night about six months ago. Rusty Nails, a band we follow, was performing. Belinda was sitting with several other women at the table next to us, and we started talking.

"She's very pretty and started flirting with him. He responded and after that evening they spent a lot of time together. For a couple of months other than at work, we didn't see much of him and when he occasionally wanted to hang out with us without her, she pouted and insisted on joining us. He finally got tired of her possessiveness and ended the relationship. I think it was about a month ago."

"Do you know where she lives and works? What about her friends?"

Melissa nodded. "She teaches at a childcare center in Pittsford. I think it's called Happy Days. She lives somewhere not too far from Noah, maybe Park Street or East Avenue? We never saw Belinda's friends again after the night we met them; I don't remember their names."

"What did you think of her?"

Ajani shrugged, "Not one of my favorite people, but as 'Lissa said, we hardly ever spent time with her."

"I wasn't crazy about her either; she was too needy," Melissa answered.

"Noah was a bit naïve when it came to women. I guess he was flattered when she came on to him at the bar. We knew about a steady girlfriend while he was in college, but other than that, I don't think he dated much.

"I didn't feel I could give him my opinion unless he asked for it. I figured the relationship would work out or it wouldn't; it wasn't my issue."

She sighed. "Do you think she killed him?"

"Until we interview her, we won't know. Did he say how she reacted when he broke up with her?"

Ajani said, "She wasn't happy and had a hard time accepting it."

"What makes you say that?"

Melissa answered, "She wouldn't leave him alone. She started showing up everywhere we went. We were at a coffee house near his apartment, and she walked in. She pretended it was a coincidence.

"He noticed her car parked outside his building one night; he could see it from his living room window. He also said she followed him once when he walked to the barbershop to get his hair cut. When he confronted her, she denied it, insisting she just happened to be walking in the same direction. Noah wasn't paranoid; if he believed she was stalking him, she was.

"I suggested he contact the police and get a restraining order, but he said he didn't think he was in danger and that if he ignored her she'd eventually stop," Ajani said.

"Did it stop?"

Melissa said, "No idea, although he hadn't said anything about her recently."

"I'm assuming you know that Noah's current assignment was to write feature stories about community leaders?"

They nodded.

"Did he reveal anything concerning about those interviews?"

Both reporters shook their heads.

It appeared they had nothing more to offer. Ed thanked them, gave each his business card, and asked them to call if they remembered anything more about the days leading up to Noah's death. After that, he walked back to Carol Smalley's office.

He asked her whether Noah had a work-related social media account. She said he used the name NoahNewsGuy on several sites. He posted links to some of his articles and newspaper-related topics. The newspaper's IT person monitored all the reporters' social media posts, and to her knowledge, there were never any threats.

He summarized his conversation with the young reporters; she verified their alibis and added her contact information to his phone. They exchanged business cards, and she handed over the USB drive.

"Thank you for meeting with me, Carol. Call me anytime if you think of something that might help us solve the case."

Carol walked with him to the entrance of the building. They shook hands and committed to staying in touch. Back in his car he called Annie with an update, then headed home.

CHAPTER 17

Ed let Gretchen out in the yard and played with her. He tossed a ball; she retrieved it. Then he tussled with her over a branch she'd found under a bush. A few minutes later, bored, she walked away and lay down on her bed on the porch.

She followed him inside when he went into his study to copy the files from the USB drive to his computer and started skimming through them. He wished he had the cell phone call logs, too. They would help with cross-referencing, but that would have to wait until the phone company released them.

He decided to take a quick break for lunch. He started for the kitchen when his phone rang.

"Hi, Ed, it's Carol Smalley. Is this a good time? I just remembered something."

"Yes. I'm home and was just about to get lunch. What's up?"

She explained. "Noah had been teaching a couple of night classes in journalism at Monroe County Community College. He started last fall. I knew about it because he asked for permission to leave a little early on the days he taught. I had no problem with it; he typically arrived earlier than normal each morning and often worked throughout the day without taking breaks.

Anyway, at the end of this year's spring term, he caught one of his students cheating during final exams.

"The college's policy is immediate dismissal, but the student pleaded for another chance. Noah couldn't give him one; he was required to report it. The student was expelled. A couple days later, he confronted Noah while he was on campus.

"He said that Noah had ruined his life and threatened he'd pay for it. Several other students pulled him away when it looked like he was going to assault him. Noah was upset about it and confided in me the next morning."

"Did he mention the student's name?"

"Yes, Taylor Madison. Noah refused to press charges. He hadn't actually been injured, but the college administration told Madison he was no longer welcome on campus, and if he came back, they'd arrest him for trespassing. After that, there seemed to be no contact between them, but I don't know that for certain."

"When did the spring term end?"

"Just before Memorial Day."

"Thank you. Any idea where to reach Madison?"

"I don't, but the college can probably give you an address and phone number."

CHAPTER 18

He called the college. When he explained why he wanted to speak with Madison, they provided his cell phone number, home address and a landline number. When the young man didn't answer his cell phone, instead of leaving a message, Ed called the landline. A woman answered.

"Madison residence, this is Alice. How may I help you?"

"Is this Mrs. Madison?"

"Speaking. If you're calling to solicit business, we're not interested. Please put us on your no-call list."

"No, that's not it. Please don't hang up. My name is Ed DeCleryk. I'm a criminal consultant working with the Lighthouse Cove police department on a murder case and would like to speak with your son, Taylor.

"I called his cell phone number but didn't leave a message. I'm hoping you can ask him to call me at his earliest convenience. I've been informed he may have known the deceased."

The woman was quiet for several seconds, then said, "This is about the death of that reporter, Noah Pierce, isn't it?"

"It is. We understand your son had a run-in with our victim after he was expelled for cheating. Do you know anything about that?"

"You don't need to talk with my son; he didn't kill your reporter. Yes, he was furious about being expelled and admitted he'd been so angry that he wanted to beat him up. Fortunately, other students stopped him; he could have gone to jail. What happened was a wake-up call for him to get his act together.

"Taylor is our only child, born late in our lives, but we've never coddled him. We told him that the reason for the expulsion was his fault, not his instructor's. We also said that if at some point he decided to go back to college, he'd have to figure out how to pay for it himself. We were not going to help this time."

"What's he doing now?"

"He's working at a microbrewery, Scrambling Bines, on Seneca Lake. He seems to be doing well. He's living with a few other young men, all college students, who have jobs at the brewery for the summer.

"He loves his job and admitted that what happened to him was for the best. He never really enjoyed the journalism classes and was considering changing majors when he got caught cheating. He's enrolled in Finger Lakes Community College as a business major for the fall term, but only part-time. He wants to continue to work at the brewery. He'd like to open his own one day."

"One more question: does your family have a boat? And do you know if he was working on Monday?"

"No, we don't own a boat; never been interested. I don't know if Madison was working on Monday but certainly feel free to call the brewery and ask to speak with the manager."

"Thank you, I won't take up any more of your time."

"Will you be contacting him?"

"I don't know. It will depend on what his manager says."

Ed had an idea. He called Brad; when he didn't answer, he left a message. Then he dialed the main switchboard at the police station. Barb confirmed the detective was still in Rochester. When he asked if Mia was in her office, she transferred the call.

"Hi, Mia. It's Ed. Do you feel comfortable helping me with something?"

"Depends on what it is and whether I can do it without Brad's okay. You know he's head honcho while Carrie's away."

"I do."

"How can I help you?"

He explained what he'd learned from the newspaper editor and his conversation with Taylor Madison's mother.

"I don't think he's our guy. Still, I'd like to verify that Madison was working at Scrambling Bines on Monday. Can you call the manager to confirm?

"I can't imagine Brad will have a problem with my making a phone call. I'll get back to you as soon as I learn anything."

Ed went back to Noah's computer and continued to browse through his files, curious if there was one with information about the illegal fishing industry. When he couldn't find anything, he figured he hadn't started the assignment yet, or it was too early in the process to have written any notes. Several minutes later, his phone rang.

"This was easy. I called and spoke with the manager. He verified that Madison worked double shifts on Sunday and Monday. He's trying to save money to pay for community college in the fall.

"Thanks, Mia. One more suspect off the list. Moving forward…."

CHAPTER 19

Ed had considered conducting face-to-face interviews with everyone the reporter interviewed for the profile series but reconsidered, realizing how long it would take and that the chance of one of them being the killer was remote. Instead, he decided to call everyone and follow up in person only if something set off his radar.

His phone rang at 4:00. "Hi, Brad."

"Hi, Ed. I got your message, and Mia filled me in on what you wanted. I'm glad she could help you. I expect you're tired; I know I am, but I'd like to meet with you around 4:30 if that works. I want to hear about your interviews and give you an update on the investigation.

"Some positive news, too. The phone company sent Noah's phone logs. I'll scan them and email you a copy."

"How about if, instead of my coming to the police station, you come here. It will be quiet; Annie won't be home until about 6:00. We can sit outside, have a beer and enjoy the view while we're talking. You don't have to wait until 4:30; come any time."

"Great! I'll be there in a few minutes."

The two men sat in the yard on Adirondack chairs facing the lake, IPAs from a local brewery in hand. A small lime green metal table with a basket of tortilla chips and a bowl of salsa lay on a tray between them.

Gretchen had been sleeping on her bed in the kitchen, but when she realized Ed was no longer in the house, she scratched the screen door and whined to be let out. As soon as she saw Brad, she ran over to him, wagged her tail and then flopped on her back for a belly rub. Ed went inside to get her bed and placed it on the grass in front of them. After a couple minutes, she lay down on it and fell asleep.

Ed summarized his conversation with Carol Smalley. "After I met with her, I spoke with two young reporters with whom he'd been friendly. They verified he'd been dating someone; her name is Belinda Corey. His parents were correct; he ended the relationship. The reporters said she was needy and possessive, and after they broke up, she started stalking him. They told me where she works. I'll follow up with a phone call. What about you?"

"I heard back from the Gananoque police chief. No surprise; the Pierces' alibi checked out."

"Did you learn anything that could help with the investigation other than what we've already discussed?"

"Yes. We viewed tapes from cameras that had been placed around his building. He was in and out on Saturday and Sunday and left his apartment yesterday morning around 4:45, which would make sense, given the timeline.

"He was carrying a messenger bag over one shoulder and sipping what we assume was coffee from a black travel mug with a white 'Yin' symbol. There was a dirty coffee pot in the sink and a filter and coffee grounds in his trash. The travel mug appears to be one of a set; we found a white one with a black 'Yang' symbol in a kitchen cabinet.

"The tapes from the camera in the front of the building recorded that someone picked him up in a newish, upscale-looking black SUV about 15 minutes later. Unfortunately, we couldn't identify the make, model, or the license plate numbers in the front or back of the vehicle. The video recorded a sideview only."

"So, he knew his killer."

"That's my guess."

Just then, Ed's phone rang. It was Carol Smalley again.

"Hi, Ed. I just thought of something else. Do you have time to talk?"

Ed sighed and rolled his eyes. He knew the editor wanted to help, but he wished she'd given him the information when he'd been at the newspaper office. He hoped the calls wouldn't become a habit. "Hi, Carol, hold on a minute. I'm here with Brad Washington. I'm going to put you on speakerphone."

A few seconds later he said, "Okay, all set. Before we begin, I wanted to let you know that Taylor Madison is in the clear; he has an alibi for the day Noah was killed, but thanks for the tip. What's up?"

"Does the name Peyton Stewart mean anything to you?"

"No. Why?"

"He's the son of our state assemblywoman, Paula Stewart, and her husband, Evan, a stockbroker."

"She doesn't represent our district, but now that you mention it, I do recognize her name. What's this about?"

"The couple has three children, two of whom turned out just fine, but Peyton has been a problem since he was in middle school. Lots of scrapes, issues with drugs, although to his parents' credit, they never bailed him out of any trouble he got into.

"He managed to graduate high school with respectable grades and attended Buffalo State University for college but dropped out after his second year and moved back to Rochester. My understanding is that since then he'd been unable to keep a steady job.

"I expect you probably don't follow Rochester news that closely, but a couple months ago Peyton was arrested in Dansville for drug dealing. He pleaded guilty to avoid a trial, but despite being offered a plea deal, refused to name his supplier. He's serving eight years at Groveland Correctional Facility in Livingston County."

"What's this have to do with our case?"

"Maybe nothing, but something happened that you should know about."

She explained that Noah had witnessed a drug deal at a neighborhood party one weekend. He'd walked by a room just as Stewart was handing out drugs to several people, and there was a large amount of cash.

"He identified Stewart from articles we'd published with photos of him and his family. He was quite upset about it and a couple of days later confided in me because he needed advice about what to do. He said he left as soon as he realized what was going on; he never would have attended in the first place if he'd suspected there would be drugs at that party.

"I wanted to keep him out of it and notified one of my contacts with the Rochester police, informing her that we'd received an anonymous tip. She thanked me but confirmed Stewart was already on their radar; he was selling drugs in several counties. A few weeks later he was apprehended.

"The reason for my call is that I'm wondering if someone who purchased drugs at that party recognized Noah, knew he was a reporter, and putting two-and-two together, assumed he alerted the authorities about Stewart."

"Carol, Stewart's in prison; he couldn't have killed Noah unless he arranged a hit."

"That's true, but remember I said he wouldn't name his supplier. What if the supplier arranged the hit?"

"Why Noah? Stewart was dealing drugs in multiple counties, and someone in Dansville might have actually been working with the police as an informant, which is how they learned about his drug dealing. That would make the most sense."

"There's something else you should know. Robert Lessley, the chamber of commerce executive, is Paula Stewart's brother. I think I told you Noah called him multiple times to schedule an interview for the Sunday profile series. Each time, Lessley blew him off, saying he was too busy to meet with him."

"I remember. Maybe he really was too busy. He has a very big job."

"I got the sense there was more to it than that. Noah said Lessley was curt with him when he called."

Ed responded, "So, putting two and two together, you have reason to believe Lessley is Stewart's supplier and killed Noah out of revenge because he lost a profitable account? I appreciate the information, but that seems like a huge stretch of the imagination. He has a prominent position in Rochester and certainly must be well paid."

"I expect he is. But we don't know his personal circumstances; maybe his salary isn't enough to support him in the way he would like, or maybe he needs money for another reason.

"I know for a fact that he's taken trips to Mexico with chamber executives from Buffalo and Syracuse; they're arranging partnerships with some of the companies located across the border from cities in Texas. Those trips would give him a conduit to arrange for the purchase of drugs."

"Have any of your sources indicated he's being investigated?"

"Not him specifically, but when I asked the same contact at the police department about it, all she would say is the supplier is on their radar, he works in a well-paid, prominent white-collar job in the city, and they're getting close to making an arrest. She refused to give me any other details."

"That certainly puts a different spin on it. I hadn't planned on interviewing any of the subjects of Noah's profile series other than with perfunctory phone calls, but I'll schedule a meeting with Lessley. I'm not optimistic he's our killer, but it doesn't hurt to rule him out."

"Please keep me posted and let me know if there's anything else I can do to help you."

"I will. Thank you."

The two ended the call.

Brad said, "I can understand why you're not sold on Lessley being Noah's killer, but at least it's a lead, Ed. Do you want me to come with you when you interview him?"

"Thanks, but I don't think it's necessary. I'm only doing this to cover all bases; I'd be remiss if I didn't."

Noticing how tired Ed looked, Brad said, "For some reason, there's been a lull in criminal activity here in the village, and Carrie will be back in a couple days. You offered to call the community leaders Noah interviewed. How about if I speak with everyone else on our list?"

"That's a generous offer, but I don't think the calls will take much time. You have responsibilities unrelated to this case."

"Ed. I'm making those calls. I insist."

Ed smiled. "How about if we split them instead? You contact Belinda Corey, Stacy Morgan and her father, and in addition to those listed for the newspaper assignment, I'll contact Noah's sister, his college friends, landlord, and neighbors."

"That's a lot, Ed."

"But unlike you, Brad, my sole focus is on this case. I can handle making those calls."

"Okay, but if you get overwhelmed and change your mind, let me know."

CHAPTER 20

Brad's cell phone rang. He answered and spoke for a few minutes, then hung up.

"That was one of the forensic techs from the crime lab. They were able to identify Noah's and Belinda Corey's prints, hair strands and fibers from his apartment and car. She works with children so she's in the system.

"There were others, most likely from friends and neighbors, but they couldn't identify those. I guess it means he probably didn't consort with known criminals." He laughed.

Ed rolled his eyes. "Brad."

"Sorry, Ed. I couldn't help myself."

"I know. You were just trying to bring a little levity into what is an otherwise depressing situation."

"True dat."

Ed barked out a laugh. "Now where did that come from?"

Brad grinned. "To alleviate some of my stress, I've been shooting hoops with our next-door neighbors' teenagers. I guess their speech rubbed off on me."

Ed laughed again. "You certainly are a man of many surprises."

Brad grinned. "To continue, as Mike suspected, the threads in his shoes were from marine carpet that's manufactured for boats, and no one else's DNA was on his body. I guess we're back to square one."

When he finished the sentence, he closed his eyes.

"Brad, you're not going back to the station when you leave here, are you? You're fading."

The young detective, startled, opened his eyes. "You're right. As you know, I was in my office at 5:00 this morning, and although I've had only one beer, I won't go back there with alcohol in my system."

"Felicia and I planned on going to dinner tonight at La Estrellita, the new Mexican restaurant on the bay, but I called her before I came over and suggested we order pizza instead. She understands; she works long hours, too. What about you?"

"We're staying in tonight. We typically don't go out for dinner on weeknights, especially during the summer when there's so much activity at the museum."

"We're going to the restaurant tomorrow night instead. Want to join us?"

"We've not been there yet, but we're having dinner with Garrett Rosenfeld and Suzanne Gordon at Rumrunners. How about if we take a raincheck and join you another time?"

"That works. We both know Suzanne and like her a lot. Neither one of us has met her husband."

"Despite being a high-profile defense attorney, he's very down to earth. You'd like him. Maybe we can schedule a time for the six of us to get together at the restaurant later this summer."

"Sounds like a plan." He yawned. "I'm going home. See you tomorrow."

CHAPTER 21

Ed carried the empty beer bottles and remaining chips and salsa inside, filled Gretchen's bowl with kibbles, and took it and a dish of water out to the porch. Although in a deep sleep, she woke when she smelled the food. Gobbling it up in two minutes, she took a huge, slurping drink then ran into the yard, squatted, did her business, raced to the back door and scratched it. She apparently had spent enough time outdoors.

Exhausted from a long and stressful day, Ed walked to his study, turned on the radio to a classical music station, sat in his leather recliner and promptly fell asleep.

He felt a hand on his shoulder and awoke, startled.

"Sorry, Ed. I came home a little early. Are you okay? It's not like you to nap during the day, and you look a little pale."

"Truth be told, I'm overwhelmed and overstimulated. Brad was here a little while ago. We each had a beer. I don't want any more alcohol, but if you'd like, I can pour you a glass of wine and we can go sit outside on the porch. I'll tell you about my long and tiring day."

Several minutes later Annie said, "I understand why you're so overwhelmed, Ed. Can you let the case go for the rest of the evening?"

"I can try. Annie, I'm wondering if I made a mistake when I agreed to help investigate this murder. When I retired as police chief and decided to become a criminal consultant, my original plan was to conduct training sessions and consult with police forces that were restructuring their departments. I never expected that most of my work would entail solving murders.

"I don't think you made a mistake. Up until now, you've really enjoyed the challenges. I'm wondering if, because Noah was so young, this case is harder for you than the others."

"That's part of it, and as a result I've been pushing myself to find his killer. I'm hoping with a good night's sleep I'll wake up tomorrow with a different perspective."

Ed changed the subject. "I'm getting hungry; how about you? I was going to grill fish for dinner, but I don't feel like cooking, and I don't expect you to cook. This might be a night to order takeout from The Brewery."

She smiled. "Or, so neither of us has to go out and pick it up, we can order a pizza and have it delivered."

"That's an even better idea."

CHAPTER 22

Ed called Noah's sister the next morning. Sobbing, she answered his questions, taking deep, shaky breaths to collect herself. She had no idea who might have murdered her brother. He seemed happy and untroubled the last time she'd spoken with him.

He also called Noah's landlord who provided him with the names of young tenants with whom the young reporter had been friendly. They confirmed they'd spent the Saturday before his death with him, picnicking on the beach at Durand-Eastman Park, and then that evening at a bar near where they lived. He was in good spirits. Their alibis checked out.

Noah's college friends confirmed that he'd been with them on Sunday in Syracuse. They ate lunch at a restaurant on Onondaga Lake, then biked the lake trail. Their alibis checked out, too.

Brad reported that when he contacted Belinda Corey, she admitted she'd been distraught when Noah had ended the relationship but denied stalking him and insisted, despite contradictory statements from his parents and friends, that if he'd lived they would have reconciled. Her supervisors verified that she'd been working at the childcare center from 6:30 AM until 3:30 PM the day of the murder.

He'd spoken with Stacy Morgan and her father. She was saddened to learn about Noah's death but had recently become engaged to a surgical resident at Upstate Medical Center in Syracuse. Her employer corroborated her alibi; she'd returned the previous evening from a three-day conference in Santa Fe, New Mexico.

Jim Morgan had recently remarried. He and his wife, a florist, had spent the morning that Noah died at a flower market in Syracuse, purchased sandwiches for lunch from a food truck there, and afterwards drove south to Cazenovia where they shopped and had an early dinner at an inn on the lake before returning to Rochester. He scanned and emailed the detective his credit card receipts.

CHAPTER 23

That evening, the DeCleryks and their friends convened at the bar at Rumrunners, as always crowded with smartly dressed patrons who were sitting on bar stools or standing in noisy clusters from one end to the other. Garrett motioned to the bartender, who took their drink orders. He suggested that instead of trying to talk above the din, they take their beverages outside.

The hostess guided them to four brightly painted Adirondack chairs that were arranged in a circle on the lawn with a sweeping view of the lake. She said she'd come for them when their table was ready.

They had just sat down when Garrett said, "I need to go back inside. I left my credit card on the bar; hopefully the bartender picked it up."

The bartender smiled when he saw the attorney and walked over to the cash register where he had placed the card.

"I just noticed it," he said. "One of the servers was going to find you and give it to you."

"Thanks, Charlie." He started walking toward the door when he felt a hand on his shoulder. Startled, he turned around and recognized an old friend, Chris Kane, and his wife, Elena. He grinned.

"Chris, Elena, how nice to see you."

The tall, slim, distinguished looking man was clean-shaven with close-cropped black hair, graying at the temples, and striking silver-blue eyes. He was wearing tan slacks, an open collared light blue Oxford shirt, navy blue sport coat, and brown tasseled loafers. A wide gold wedding band encircled his left ring finger.

His tiny wife's wavy dark brown hair cascaded down to her shoulders, her huge almond-shaped long-lashed brown eyes sparkled with humor and warmth. She was wearing a short, sleeveless black linen dress, black patent leather sandals, a slim diamond wedding band and a trio of gold circle bracelets.

Garrett hugged them. "It's been ages," he said. "Suzanne and I are here with our friends Ed and Annie DeCleryk from Lighthouse Cove. She runs the historical society and museum there and he established a criminal consultant practice after retiring as the village's police chief. We're having drinks before dinner outside by the water. Join us?"

"I'd love to. What about you, Elena?"

"Me, too," she replied. "We have plenty of time; our reservation isn't until 7:45."

As soon as Suzanne saw the Kanes approach, she sprang from her chair and hugged them. "It's been way too long."

Garrett grabbed two chairs that had been recently vacated, placed them into the circle and introduced them to Ed and Annie.

He said, "Chris and Elena are old friends. We bumped into each other at the bar. I hope you don't mind my inviting them to sit with us."

"Of course not. Welcome," Annie said. Ed nodded and smiled.

Chris said, "Nice to meet you both, too. Annie, Garrett said that you run the historical society and museum in Lighthouse Cove, and Ed, that you're a criminal consultant."

"That's correct," Ed replied.

"How did all of you meet?" Elena asked.

Annie explained how she and Suzanne had forged a friendship when the younger woman served on her board of directors, and that Ed and Garrett had bonded immediately when the two women introduced them at a party.

She asked, "And how do the four of you know each other?"

Garrett responded that he and Chris both attended Cornell Law School, although not at the same time. He was a decade older; they'd met at a cocktail party that was hosted by the Rochester chapter of the college's alumni association and hit it off immediately.

"But our careers went in different directions. We frequently see each other in court but we're on opposite sides." Chris grinned.

"I was wondering why your name is so familiar," Annie said. "Now I remember. I've seen you being interviewed on TV. You're the Monroe County district attorney."

"I am."

Elena said, "Garrett introduced us. I was clerking at his law office, and he said he had a friend he wanted me to meet. It was love at first sight. We've been married for twenty years."

"Are you still a defense attorney?" Ed asked her.

"No. As it turned out, it really wasn't a great fit for me. I started dabbling in art, mixed media, initially to relieve stress. But I appeared to have a talent for it, and after a couple years, I started to exhibit at some galleries in the city. I still exhibit, but now I mostly create to get away from the pressures of being the mom of four."

"How old are your kids?" Annie asked.

"Fifteen, thirteen, eleven and seven. Two of each; they keep us plenty busy. What about you?"

"Two married sons and five grandchildren. One family lives in Maryland, and the other in Ohio."

"You're fortunate to live in Lighthouse Cove; it's a charming village," Chris said.

Annie responded, "It is, and we love being on the water."

"Do you live on the bay near Suzanne and Garrett?" Elena asked.

"No, we're on the lake. When we moved from Albany after Ed was hired as police chief, we purchased a ship captain's house that was built in the mid-1800s. It wasn't in great shape, but with a lot of love and a huge dent in our finances, we were able to bring back the character of the place with modern conveniences."

"Annie's a great cook, and she and Ed are wonderful hosts. We've spent many nights enjoying her delicious meals and watching the sunset from their backyard," Garrett remarked.

"We'll have to get you over to the house for dinner sometime with Suzanne and Garrett, hopefully before the season ends."

"We'd enjoy that. Elena and I own a cottage on White Pelican Island; we spend a lot of summer weekends there with our kids. If the weather cooperates, instead of driving, we could sail our boat to the village. Do you have a dock?"

"No, we're on a bluff, and the beach beneath us is too rocky."

"You could use the dock behind our house and walk with us to Annie and Ed's. One of the nice things about living in a small village is that everything is so close," Suzanne said.

"We'll look at some dates and get back to you," Annie said and changed the subject. "Have you met our good friends Eve and Henri Beauvoir? They used to live on White Pelican Island but recently downsized to move a couple blocks from us."

Elena responded, "Their names aren't familiar. When we're there, we're usually too busy with family activities to socialize much with our neighbors."

Chris looked at Ed. "I heard about Noah Pierce's body being found at Chimney Bluffs; horrible situation. Are you helping to investigate?"

Ed said, "I am. What happened to him is unbelievably tragic. I understand he was planning to interview you and a family member for a series he was writing for the newspaper."

"That's correct. My staff and I are in the middle of preparing for a trial. When we spoke, he agreed to postpone the interview until it gets started. I'll have more time then; two assistant DAs will be prosecuting that case.

"Initially, Noah also planned to interview my father, who took over the reins as CEO of the company my grandfather started when he retired several years ago. My parents are away on a lengthy cruise.

"Dad convinced Grandpa to fill in for him until they get back. He agreed to speak with Noah, but I don't think Noah contacted him yet. I check in with him every day, and he hasn't said anything about it."

He paused. "Although it's possible he forgot to mention it to me. He's in his late 80s and his memory isn't always as sharp as it used to be."

"I'm calling everyone who agreed to be interviewed for the series. I have no reason to believe any of you were involved in his murder; it's just routine."

"I understand. You're going to want our alibis for the morning he died. To save you time, I had a staff meeting at the diner across the street from the courthouse at 7:30 a.m.; any of my staff can verify that.

"I'll be seeing my grandfather tomorrow. Elena needs a little time to herself; he and I are taking the kids to a baseball game. I'll let him know you'll be calling him, too."

His wife smiled. "It's a little frantic at our house this time of year. Four active kids give me little time to paint or do anything for myself. I'll be glad for the break."

Chris continued, "Grandpa normally plays golf on Saturday, but our children pleaded with him to join us for the game, and he can't say no to them."

"You're lucky to have grandparents who are still alive," Suzanne said. "Mine were all gone by the time I was in my late 20s."

"Yes, I am. Despite their being in their 80s, Grandpa and Grandma Kane are still relatively healthy, although his mind is not quite as sharp as it used to be."

CHAPTER 24

Annie asked Elena if she knew their friend, Jon Bradford, the owner of a sculpture gallery in the city. His first wife, Emily, had worked at the museum's gift shop and had become a dear friend.

"Ed and I stayed in contact with Jon after she died, and as much as I miss Emily, we adore his second wife, Stephanie."

Elena said, "I do know Jon, and Stephanie and I go way back. When I was in law school at SUNY Buffalo, I took some painting classes at an art studio where she was teaching glass sculpture. We became friends but lost contact after I moved to Rochester. I recently bumped into her at an art supply store here, and we've resumed the friendship.

"Were you aware that Jon's planning to expand the gallery? He's asked me to exhibit some of my paintings there when the addition is completed."

Ed responded, "We were. When Annie and I had dinner with Jon and Stephanie a few weeks ago, he told us about it."

"I'll make sure all of you receive an invitation to my opening reception, although it probably won't be until later this summer or sometime in the fall."

The group made small talk for several more minutes, and at 7:30 the hostess appeared, announced that the Rosenfeld table was ready, and that the Kane's table would be available soon.

Garrett invited Chris and Elena to join them, certain the server could add two chairs to their table, but the couple declined, indicating that with their very busy lives, they were looking forward to a quiet meal by themselves.

There were handshakes and hugs, then Garrett, Suzanne, Ed and Annie were escorted to a corner table in the main dining room with a splendid view of the lake. The owner had recently remodeled; the walls were covered with grass cloth and hung with abstract watercolors in subdued maritime hues. Lovely contemporary chandeliers and wall sconces made of brass and opaque glass lit the room.

They ordered two bottles of wine, red and white, and an appetizer. When it arrived, they placed their meal orders.

"What a nice couple," Annie remarked.

"They are. We really enjoy their company," Garrett answered, "but it's been ages since we've spent time with them; we never seem to be able to coordinate our schedules. There's been some talk that Chris might run for New York attorney general. He's well-regarded, and I'd back him in a heartbeat. He's one of the most unassuming guys I've ever met; nothing phony about him. I really respect him."

Curious, Ed asked, "What's his background?"

"You'd never know it from talking with him, but the family is quite wealthy. Chris is a trust fund baby, but he doesn't take his wealth for granted. His parents insisted he and his sister work part-time when they were in college; unlike some kids from privileged families, they had summer jobs, too.

"Greg and Cheryl wanted their children to understand the value of money. Chris and Elena decided early on that, with a few exceptions, they were going to live within their means. They're not frivolous at all."

"They seem very down to earth," Ed remarked.

"They are. Chris' parents and grandparents live in lovely homes in upper middle-class neighborhoods in Rochester, but neither is a mansion. Chris and Elena live along the lake in Webster in a rambling, old clapboard built in the 1930s, but there's nothing ostentatious about it.

"What Elena didn't tell you about their cottage on the island is that it's part of a large family compound; his grandparents, parents, aunts, uncles, and sister and her family also own places there, all with boat houses. It's located on the northern tip, overlooking the lake.

"None of the cottages is overly large, and they're all decorated for comfort, and kid and pet friendly. A converted barn serves as a gathering place for parties and holiday celebrations. Like the cottages, it's not pretentious."

"Where's the money come from?" Annie asked.

"Global transportation—shipping, overland, air. His grandfather, Desmond, is a self-made man who started as a driver for a trucking company, worked his way up to an executive position, and eventually bought the company and expanded it. They now do business internationally."

"Of course, KGT. Kane Global Transport. I've seen the name on freighters at the Pier of Rochester and on railroad cars and trucks," Annie replied.

"The family doesn't seek attention. They contribute millions to charity but often as anonymous donors. Wings at hospitals, symphony endowments, animal shelters; that sort of thing.

"Like his son and grandson, Desmond is quite humble. He avoids the limelight; won't do interviews and credits his family and those who have worked for the company for its success."

"If he's that unassuming, it's amazing he agreed to let Noah speak with him," Ed said.

"That's different. He'd do anything for his family."

"What's Elena's background?" Annie asked.

Suzanne replied, "Her father's family emigrated from India a couple of generations back; her mother's family came from Italy around the same time. Elena grew up in Bethesda, Maryland; her parents are both researchers for NIH.

"She has two siblings who work for the government, too, and also live in Bethesda. She and her family are close; they often visit here during the summer, and she, Chris and their kids make frequent trips to Maryland."

Their meals arrived; they ate and chatted amiably. Just before dusk, the sky turned pink and purple, and the sun, making its final descent to the horizon, cast shimmering rays of molten gold across the lake. For several minutes, they watched without speaking, appreciating the staggering beauty in front of them.

Their server brought coffee and dessert. They had just finished when Andy Spurling, the restaurant owner, sauntered over to their table.

CHAPTER 25

"Good evening, everyone." A tall man of medium build with hazel eyes, short sandy hair flecked with gray, and a goatee, greeted his guests. He was wearing loosely fitting ivory linen slacks, a silk open-collared black shirt, and polished black loafers without socks. "I hope you enjoyed your meals."

"Oh, hi, Andy. As usual, the food and service were exceptional. We just finished," Annie responded.

"If you're ready, come with me. I think you're going to love seeing what I found. Ed, Garrett and Suzanne, you're welcome to join us."

"I wish we could, but I'm leading a yoga group on the beach tomorrow morning at 6:30. I think we better get going. I'm looking forward to hearing all about it, Annie. If it's not too late, text me," Suzanne responded.

The server approached and placed the bill on the table. Garrett took a card out of his wallet and handed it to her. Ed started to get his card out of his wallet, too, but Garrett said to put it away; he and Suzanne were treating them.

"It's not necessary," Ed responded.

"You've entertained us at your house more times than we can count. We insist; it's our pleasure. Don't argue."

Ed said, "We never expected this, but thank you."

Annie hugged her friends. "Yes, thank you."

The restaurateur led Annie and Ed into a large banquet room that was mainly used during holidays for overflow seating. He walked over to a door along the far wall, opened it, and turned on a light that revealed another room, almost as large, that was filled with stacked tables and chairs, and along one wall, a large wooden cabinet.

"We think this was part of the original structure. It's over 100 years old, and the restaurant you see today was expanded around it. We currently use it for storage, but our plan is to knock down the walls between these two rooms, which will give us more space for banquets and special events.

"As you know, rumor has it that the restaurant had once been the site of a speakeasy, but we never found proof other than a few bar stools we discovered in a closet after we bought the place.

He walked to the cabinet and started to move it aside.

Ed said, "Andy, let me help you with that; it looks heavy."

"Thanks, it's on gliders; I've done this before."

The wall behind the cabinet revealed another door. He opened it and turned on a light that illuminated narrow stone steps, but they couldn't see what was at the bottom.

"We didn't know this was here until we moved the cabinet. The steps are not in great shape. I'll go first and turn on the light down there. Be careful; I don't want you to fall and injure yourselves."

CHAPTER 26

The walls were thick stone, whitewashed with crumbling stucco, and the floor, age-distressed brick. At the far end of the room stood a long wooden bar and stools with cracked upholstered leather seats and rusted metal legs. Behind it, empty shelves were affixed to a gold-flecked mirror. Beside it hung a faded, painted sign, proclaiming *Tony's Place*.

Several round oak tables sat atop iron pedestals, each surrounded by four wooden captain's chairs. Frosted glass art deco sconces had been strategically placed around the perimeter of the room. A small, raised stage, big enough for a jazz combo, had been constructed in one corner of the room, with a small, triangular dance floor in front of it.

"Oh my, Andy, I can't believe what we're seeing. It's a speakeasy, isn't it?"

Andy nodded. "It is. We had no idea it was here, and no surprise, it was a mess. We cleaned up mouse droppings, cobwebs, dead insects, rodents, and layers of dust. As you know, the inlet on the east side of the restaurant was where rumrunners unloaded their contraband liquor during Prohibition, so it all makes sense. It appears the proprietor left hastily, although your guess is as good as mine as to why."

He walked behind the bar, bent down to a shelf and retrieved a dark brown glass bottle along with a rum barrel with the word 'RUM' etched on the front dated 1925, then handed it to her.

"He left something behind. It's yours for the museum if you can use it."

"Oh my, of course I can! I'm not sure I mentioned it, but our next exhibit will be about the Prohibition era and rumrunning on the lake. This will fit perfectly. Thank you." She handed it to Ed, who examined it, looking impressed.

"Andy, instead of expanding the space upstairs have you considered restoring all of this and opening a speakeasy? I suspect your patrons would love it. I know we would."

He responded that he'd initially considered it, but the expansion would allow them to increase the number of bookings for special events which made more sense from a business standpoint.

"We need to remove all of this soon. The contractors plan to start construction within the next few weeks and want to use this space to build a new foundation under the rooms above. I'd like to donate everything in here that can be disassembled and reassembled to the museum if you can find space for it."

Annie stood on tiptoe and hugged the restaurateur. "Oh my, this certainly is a wonderful surprise. When we relocated the Abolition Movement and Underground Railroad exhibit to Macyville, I considered turning the exhibit space into a conference room, but our boardroom serves that purpose, so it didn't make a lot of sense.

"Then I thought about turning it into a gallery for local artists, but we already have a couple in the village, and I didn't want to compete with them. Now I know exactly what I'll do. I had planned for the next exhibit to be fairly small; a few artifacts like this bottle, perhaps some photos, paintings and a brochure about that period of time. Instead, we'll use the space to recreate the speakeasy. We can make it a permanent exhibit. Our visitors will love it."

"How will you get all of this out of here? The steps are awfully narrow," Ed asked.

"The tabletops can be unscrewed from the bases and, along with the chairs, bar stools and sconces, can easily be carried up the steps. Our contractor thinks he can remove the sign without damaging it, disassemble the bar and put it back together; ditto for the shelves and the stage. Unfortunately, the mirror is too fragile to remove from the wall, and he won't be able to save the dance floor."

Annie said, " It will take work and some expense, but I'm sure we can restore everything to almost its original condition. The only concern I have is what to do with the pieces we can't use. Our exhibit space is only big enough for about half of this."

"What if we take the other pieces to an antique consignment shop? The proceeds from the sales could be donated to the museum," Andy suggested.

"That's a good idea, but I just thought of something else. We can auction the remaining items at our upcoming fundraising gala. Since the theme is the 1920s, it's a perfect fit, and I think we'll raise a lot of money. I'll send a broadcast email with photos attached to our members to announce it."

"I'd like to get all of it out of here in a week or two, before the construction starts. I'll hire a moving company to transport the items you want for the exhibit, but what do you want to do with the ones for the gala?"

"We don't have room for them at the museum. Is there any way you can store them for us?"

"I can't, but I'd be happy to rent storage space and hire someone to bring them to the club for the gala."

Annie had an idea. "Have you met Elena and Chris Kane? They're friends of Suzanne and Garrett and joined us for drinks before dinner tonight."

"They're regular customers here, too. I noticed they were sitting outside with you earlier this evening. Why?"

She replied that she was wondering if Chris' grandfather would be willing to send a crew from Kane Global Transport to deliver the pieces to the museum and store the others for them at one of their warehouses until the gala.

"I could call Elena and ask. Garrett said the family is quite philanthropic."

"Annie, that would really help. If they agree, let me know the details, and I'll arrange for a time to meet them. If it doesn't work out, we'll go to plan A and rent the storage space."

He walked over to a door next to the shelves where the liquor had been and opened it. Two wooden filing cabinets stood on the floor.

"These are empty except for a few old menus; you could frame them and put them on a wall. Would you be interested in taking the cabinets, too?"

"Not for the exhibit, but we might be able to auction them off, along with the other pieces. Thank you so much; this is an amazing find and a wonderful surprise." She reached up and hugged the restaurateur again.

They walked back upstairs, Andy into the dining room to greet other diners, and the DeCleryks to the bar where they ordered snifters of brandy. With drinks in hand, they wandered into an adjacent room and sat at a table for two to listen to a musician playing American Songbook standards on a grand piano.

While Annie texted Suzanne, Ed strolled over to the piano player and whispered something in his ear. He nodded, grinned and a few minutes later started playing *Time After Time*, one of the couple's favorite songs. Ed took Annie's hand and led her onto the small dance floor while the other patrons looked on, amused. She laughed and rolled her eyes.

CHAPTER 27

Annie was unusually subdued on the way home. Ed glanced over to her and and said, "Annie, we just had a lovely evening with friends, and the speakeasy is an amazing find, but since we left Rumrunners you've been very quiet. What's troubling you?"

"I've been thinking about Noah and how lucky we are, Ed. Our sons and their families are healthy and safe. If one of them was murdered I don't know how I'd cope. I barely knew him; we only spoke twice, but I feel so sad about his death. He was young, bright and had an amazing future ahead of him. He should be enjoying life right now instead of being mourned by those who love him."

"Understandable."

"Ed, for some reason my instincts are telling me that the fire that killed his ancestor, the speakeasy and his murder are connected. I have no idea how or why, but I intend to find out."

"Annie, I've learned over the years to trust you. But you do know that we have to explore every lead, even those that have nothing to do with what happened to his ancestor or the speakeasy."

"Of course you do, Ed. And despite what I just said, I could be completely off base."

"What's your plan?"

"I'm going to retrace Noah's steps at the library and am hoping at the same time to see if I can discover anything about the speakeasy and who Tony was. Initially, I thought I'd wait until fall when things slow down at the museum, but instead, I've decided to start next week. I'll share whatever I learn with you, of course, but also with his parents. They deserve to know the truth."

"Are you sure you want to add more to your plate right now? You don't have a lot of time to spare."

"I promoted Jason, so I don't have to be at the museum 24/7. He's perfectly capable of handling anything that comes up while I'm at the library. I'll only be gone for an hour or so, at the most once or twice a week. If there's a problem he can't solve, he'll know how to reach me, and I'll only be a few minutes away."

"Then I think it's a great idea. I'd be happy to pick up the slack at home; maybe do a bit more cooking and caring for Gretchen."

"You already do more than your share, Ed. This isn't going to be stressful, just a little time-consuming."

Ed parked the car in the garage. They changed into jeans, tee shirts and sneakers, walked Gretchen around the block, then read for a while in bed before turning off the lights. That night, Annie dreamed she was a flapper, wearing a short, beaded dress with fringe at the bottom, drinking fizzy rum drinks and dancing the Lindy Hop with Ed in a speakeasy called *Tony's Place*.

CHAPTER 28

The next morning, while Annie was at the museum conducting a training session for new docents, Ed began looking through Noah's cell phone calls, comparing the numbers to the contacts in his computer. He wasn't surprised that there had been several between the reporter and the chamber of commerce executive, the most recent a week before his death.

He decided to wait until Monday to continue working on the case. Happy to have a little time to himself, he drove to the marina to clean the pontoon, completing the task just before noon. Returning home, he fixed himself a ham and cheese sandwich and, with a biography of Abraham Lincoln, headed out to the porch when his phone rang. It was Annie.

"Hi. I'm heading to the garden club luncheon at Fitzhugh House in a few minutes. I don't have much time, but I have news. Can you talk?"

"I can. I worked on the case for a while, then decided to pack it in for the weekend. I spent most of the morning cleaning the boat. What's up?"

She replied, "I was too excited to wait until next week to call Elena to ask if she'd be willing to speak with Chris' grandfather about moving and storing the speakeasy items for us. I texted Suzanne; she sent me her cell phone number."

"I just got off the phone with her. She was happy to hear from me; she said she and Chris had enjoyed meeting us and hoped that we all could get together again soon. I said we felt the same way and then told her why I was calling. She promised to talk with her father-in-law tonight; she and Chris' grandmother are meeting the rest of the family for dinner after the baseball game.

"She called back a few minutes ago. Instead of waiting, she texted him indicating she had something to discuss with him that evening. As soon as he got the text, Desmond called her. The game was boring and he was glad to take a break. When she explained what she wanted, he said he'd be delighted to help."

"Great news. What a generous man."

"Generous family. I got his address from Elena and will send him a thank-you note. I'm very appreciative of what he's doing.

"Anyway, before we ended the call, she mentioned that she'd never visited the museum and at some point would like to see it. Monday's an easy day for me. She's coming in; I'll take her on the tour and then treat her to lunch at Bistro Louise."

"Seems like you're starting a nice, new friendship, Annie."

"I think so, too. I like both her and Chris a lot and am looking forward to spending more time with them. Anyway, I wanted to share the news with you before heading out to Fitzhugh House. Have a relaxing afternoon; I'll see you in a few hours. Kisses."

CHAPTER 29

The circa 1812 home, with its antique china and silver, splendid Neoclassical furniture, silk Oriental rugs and original American primitive folk art, had been bequeathed to the historical society after the sudden passing of the owner, Amanda Reynolds. It now served as a gathering place for community organizations to host small group special events.

In the dining room, guests helped themselves to a light buffet of sandwiches, salads, and an assortment of cookies and cold beverages. Plates in hand, they strolled outside to tables that were scattered throughout the large backyard, admiring the colorful gardens, stone and ceramic sculptures, and plump, spotted fish swimming lazily in a well-maintained koi pond filled with pink waterlilies.

A podium had been placed at one end for the guest speaker, Rose Bloom, a botanist and professor at Cornell University. The title of her presentation was *Lovely or Lethal: Plants That Cure or Kill.*

Annie had laughed when she learned the speaker's name during the garden club planning session and mischievously asked if she'd changed it because of her profession. She was sitting next to Eve, who rolled her eyes and poked her elbow into Annie's side.

"*No,*" she was informed archly by the president, who was a childhood friend of the professor, "*that is her given name.*"

Annie attempted to look nonplused by the rebuke but couldn't stop grinning. She stopped herself from asking for Rose's middle initial. If it had been "N" she wouldn't have been able to contain herself.

Fixing herself a plate of food, she strolled outside and wandered over to a table where Eve was sitting with several other women, including Holly Corcoran, the village's head librarian.

The women warmly welcomed her and invited her to join them. They immediately asked about Noah Pierce's death and whether there had been any leads.

Between bites of her sandwich, Annie summarized what the investigators knew, but that at this point there were no suspects.

She turned to the librarian and asked, "Holly, will you be at the library on Monday? I don't want to go into detail now; it would take too long and I don't want to monopolize the conversation, but I want to do some research and am going to need your advice about where to start."

"I'll be there all morning. What time?"

"Probably about 9:00."

"I'll meet you at the front desk."

The program was about to begin. The speaker walked around the garden as she spoke, portable mic in hand, pointing out plants, flowers and herbs that, in small doses were medicinal, but could also kill if administered improperly. Annie's thoughts went to Amanda Reynolds, who had tended the garden with passion and malicious intent.

She stayed to help clean up and arrived home by late afternoon. Ed suggested they take the pontoon out for a cruise around the bay. He'd gone to Oldman's Farm Market and purchased an assortment of Amish cheeses, sliced ham, a crispy baguette, pickles, freshly made potato salad, and for dessert, two chocolate chip cookies.

Tired from a long and stimulating day, Annie hugged and kissed her considerate husband and quickly changed into casual attire. An hour later, Ed anchored the boat near Eagle Island on the bay, where they ate, drank wine and avoided discussing the murder case.

CHAPTER 30

Early the next morning on his way to meet with Brad and Carrie, who was now back from Canada, Ed stopped at Bistro Louise and purchased three raspberry muffins, black coffee for himself and Brad, and an iced espresso with whipped cream for the police chief. The sweet, caffeinated drinks she craved never seemed to add pounds to her slim frame.

"Welcome back, Carrie," he said as he handed out the beverages and muffins. "You look well-rested."

She beamed. "We had a fabulous time. This is the first vacation we've taken by ourselves since the kids were born. With Matt now the head of the hospital's emergency department and my crazy schedule, it's been hard finding time to get away."

The young police chief, light brown hair pulled into a ponytail, was dressed in her signature attire: brown low-top boots, khaki pants, a white, collared button-down shirt and a navy blazer. Today, because of the heat, her sleeves were rolled up to her elbows and she'd draped the blazer on the back of her desk chair.

"I know it's early days but tell me what you've accomplished so far."

The investigators summarized their progress and plans to move forward.

Ed said, "This may take a while. Noah's newspaper assignments included working on a series about community leaders, and one where he was going to investigate illegal commercial fishing on the lake, although we don't have evidence he started that yet.

"Then there's his research at the library about the fire that killed an ancestor during Prohibition, or his death may have been the result of something more personal. We'd be remiss if we didn't explore every one of those angles as a motive for killing him."

"It appears you have your work cut out for you. Let's meet every couple of days, unless something happens where you need my input or a background check or warrant. I have lots of catching up to do."

"Promoting Brad doesn't mean you're planning to leave us, does it?" Ed asked, only partially serious.

Carrie laughed and Brad grinned.

"Ed, you do recall that my parents moved here last year and bought the house next door to us, and that Matt's parents plan on relocating to Lighthouse Cove after they retire? With their support and Brad's promotion, I feel like I finally can take some time off without feeling guilty. I love my job; there's almost nothing that could entice me to leave right now. Guess you're stuck with me, and hopefully Brad, for a while."

He patted her on the shoulder. "Good to hear. I kind of like having you both around."

CHAPTER 31

While they typically didn't entertain much in the summer because of Annie's busy schedule, the couple decided to invite their friend, Sally Wright, and her companion, Kevin Greeley, to join them for an early dinner that night. Sally's husband, George, who had also been a childhood friend of Ed's, had been murdered a few years back. Ed, with help from Annie, had solved the case.

The widow had been reclusive during an intense grieving period, but then about a year ago, began venturing out with close friends and family. She'd been introduced to the retired accountant, also a widower, at a holiday party in December. They had been together ever since. Ed still mourned the loss of his good friend, but he and Annie were delighted that she'd found someone with whom to share her life.

After he returned home from his meeting, Ed walked Gretchen while Annie cooked, then went outside to set the dining table in the yard and a bar on the porch where he placed bottles of scotch and bourbon, one each of Sauvignon Blanc and dry Rosé, and a tray with a bowl of red bell pepper dip, crudités and seed crackers.

Their friends arrived at 5:00; the couples stood and chatted for several minutes while Ed poured drinks. Then Annie scurried into the kitchen to put finishing touches on the meal. Sally followed her, asking if she could help.

Annie replied that everything was under control, but she was glad to have time alone with her. She inquired about her daughter, Lily, a graphic artist, her husband, Eric, a history professor at the University of Rochester, and their two children.

"They're doing quite well. Lexi and Jack keep them really busy with all their activities. You remember how much energy elementary school-aged kids have."

"I certainly do. Our grandkids are a bit older than yours, but they were a handful when they were that age, too, and you and I both remember what our own kids were like."

By now, the men had wandered inside and had been listening to the conversation.

Changing the subject, Sally said, "I was sorry to hear about the death of that news reporter. Ed, are you involved with the investigation?"

"I am."

"Have you made any progress finding the killer?"

"No, but it's early days."

"It's just so tragic."

"It is. He was very young."

"Eric said he ran into the young man's fiancée, a former student of his, at the supermarket; he said she was devastated."

Ed said, "That's odd. No one I've interviewed said anything to me about a fiancée. Did Eric mention her name?"

"He may have; I don't remember. Do you still have his contact information? I'm sure he'd be happy to talk with you."

"I do. I'll call him next week."

"Please don't be offended, Sally, but perhaps we could change the subject. Ed's been working hard on the case and needs a break," Annie said.

"My apologies. I, of all people, should know how stressful a murder investigation can be," her friend responded.

CHAPTER 32

At 5:45, the couples sat down to a light summery meal: seafood quiche, mixed greens and mushroom salad, and for dessert, pound cake with strawberry sauce and Chantilly cream.

After dinner they brought the dishes into the kitchen and loaded the dishwasher, then strolled back outside for coffee, talking quietly.

Their friends left a short while later to drive back to Rochester. After walking Gretchen, the DeCleryks settled into the den for the rest of the evening, Ed working on a crossword puzzle, and Annie reading a mystery about a woman named Phyrne Fisher, who worked as a private detective in 1920s Australia.

Within minutes of opening her book, Annie fell asleep. Ed couldn't seem to concentrate on the puzzle, and despite his pledge to take the weekend off, quietly walked into his study and opened his computer to Noah's files.

He perused those the young reporter had written about the community leaders, with comments from families and friends; it didn't appear that any of the questions were contentious or the interviews hostile. He'd start making phone calls on Monday and schedule time to meet with Robert Lessley.

Half an hour later, he shut down his computer and walked out of his study and back to the den. Annie awoke, a little groggy. She looked at Ed and said, "Sorry, I guess I was more tired than I thought."

"It's okay. I couldn't concentrate on the crossword puzzle, and despite my pledge not to work on the case this weekend, I read some of Noah's files. I didn't find anything that would help solve his murder."

Annie said, "You must have been really surprised when Sally mentioned her conversation with Eric about Noah having a fiancée."

"I was, and the revelation puts a whole new spin on the investigation. I wonder if there's a pattern here. Noah seemed to be attracted to needy and manipulative women; Belinda Corey was also a stalker.

"Maybe after he broke up with her, he jumped into another relationship, proposed marriage but quickly regretted his decision and ended it. But this one was even more unhinged than Belinda, and when he jilted her, she went one step further and killed him. His friends at the newspaper said he didn't date much and was shy. I suppose he could have just been naïve, but it also appears he made bad choices."

"I'm not buying it, Ed; there must be something else going on. Sally may have misunderstood. When you call Eric, I'm sure he'll clear things up."

"I hope so. You know what, I'm ready for bed. What about you?"

"Me, too. It's been a long but lovely day, and I'm so happy that Sally has found someone special to share her life with."

CHAPTER 33

On Monday morning, a chorus of birds awakened Annie just as the sun was rising in the east, an abstract canvas of rose, blue and white splashing the sky.

Not wanting to disturb Ed, she quietly pulled on a robe, and with Gretchen by her side, walked downstairs to start coffee for him and brew herself a cup of tea. She let Gretchen out and fed her, tricking her into taking thyroid and arthritis pills by hiding them in a wad of peanut butter in her kibbles.

By then, Ed, yawning, had ambled into the kitchen. He kissed his wife, petted the dog and then reached gratefully for the cup of coffee she handed to him.

"I didn't mean to sleep so long. It was a good weekend, and so nice that we had absolutely nothing on our plates yesterday, but I'm still tired. What about you? How's your day look?" he asked.

"I feel a little more rested; fortunately, we don't have any large group tours scheduled. I think I mentioned to you that I'm going to the library this morning to meet with Holly Corcoran to start my research, and after that come back to the museum to take Elena on a tour and to lunch at the bistro."

"You did. Sounds like a nice day."

She asked, "What are your plans?"

"I'll call Eric and some of the community leaders on Noah's list, including one I'm going to interview. After that I'm not sure."

"Is Brad helping you?"

"Probably not today. With less responsibility now that Carrie's back, he'll have more time to work on other police business."

Her blue eyes shining, Annie said, "I'm so happy about his promotion. He deserves it, but I hope after a couple years he doesn't leave us to become a police chief somewhere else. You know how fond I am of him and Felicia; I'm not quite ready to lose them."

"I asked about that when he and I met with Carrie on Saturday. He didn't respond, but my sense is he'll stick around until he gets a bit more experience but eventually move on to become police chief somewhere else."

She grinned. "I must admit, while I think you are just about the handsomest man in the universe, he's a close second."

Ed rolled his eyes.

"I may be old, Ed, but I still can look, and you have to admit he's model gorgeous."

He laughed, patted her on the head and said, "Now that we've covered that, I think I'll go take a shower. Want to join me?"

She swatted at him. "Not now, handsome, but hold that thought. I need to get ready for work and head over to the library."

CHAPTER 34

Ed called Eric Klein. His mother-in-law had accurately reported their conversation.

"Are you comfortable sharing her name with me? This is a new development. I'd like to speak with her."

"Her name is Belinda Corey. She was a student of mine several years ago."

Ed groaned and thought, "*Annie was right, and here we go again. This woman sounds completely unhinged. She can't seem to let go of the fact that Noah ended the relationship. I should have thought of that.*"

He said, "I can't go into details about the investigation, Eric, but Noah Pierce and Belinda Corey were never engaged. In fact, he had broken up with her, and after that, she started stalking him. Initially she was a suspect, but her alibi checked out."

Eric paused for a few seconds and then said, "Ed, this just doesn't fit with what I know about her. She was an excellent student and seemed to have her act together. She had a nice group of friends, too. I'm a good judge of character, and there's nothing I ever observed that indicated she was emotionally unbalanced."

"How odd."

"Are you going to speak with her again?"

"I don't know. A background check should give me enough information to determine next steps. I expect you're not the only one she told about being engaged. She may have just needed sympathy and attention, or there's more to the story. I'm glad Sally mentioned your conversation with her."

"Good luck, Ed. As I remember from when you investigated my father-in-law's death, this could be a lengthy process."

The two men ended their call. Ed called Carrie and asked for the background check.

"How far do you want me to dig? It could take a while."

"Go deep. I want to know who her parents are, her financial situation, if she recently purchased or rented a boat, the kind of car she drives, whether a large sum of money has been recently taken from a bank account or if there have been large charges on credit cards."

"You're wondering if she's so unbalanced that she paid for someone to take him out?"

"It's a stretch, but yes I am."

"I'll get back to you as soon as I learn anything."

"Thanks, Carrie."

CHAPTER 35

Ed phoned Desmond Kane. When he'd checked Noah's call log, it appeared the industrialist may have been one of the last on the list to have spoken with the young reporter before he was killed.

Kane answered after two rings. He said he was aware that Ed would be calling; his grandson had mentioned it to him.

"Chris said he and Elena really enjoyed meeting you and your wife at Rumrunners and that they were hoping to get together again later this summer."

"The feeling is mutual. They are a delightful couple and our friends Suzanne Gordon and Garrett Rosenfeld are quite fond of them. And by the way, my wife, Annie, is very appreciative that you've agreed to move the speakeasy items to the museum and store the others for her until the gala."

"We're happy to help; it's for a good cause. I admit it's been years since my wife and I visited your museum, and I expect since then much has changed. We'll have to try to get there sometime this summer."

"If you call Annie in advance and let her know when you're coming, I suspect she'll offer to take you on a guided tour."

"I appreciate that, but this must be a busy time for her, and we wouldn't want to impose. I think we'll just stop by sometime when we're at our lake house. I'll ask for her, but we're perfectly content to take a self-guided tour if she isn't available."

He changed the subject. "My granddaughter-in-law tells me she's spending time with your wife today. Mary Elizabeth and I would like to meet you, too. You have a standing invitation to visit us when our family is at our home on the island."

"Thank you, we'd like that. Listen, I know you're a busy man, and I appreciate your taking time to speak with me. I have some questions pertaining to Noah Pierce's murder."

Ed asked Desmond if he remembered the two conversations he had with Noah the week before he died. He assured him he wasn't a suspect.

"I understand your questions are routine, Ed. No offense taken; I want to cooperate. Noah called the first time to ask if I would be willing to be interviewed for the piece about Chris in the newspaper. Although I don't normally like speaking with the press, I agreed. I'd do anything for my grandson."

"What about the second time?"

"It was kind of spur of the moment; he called late the Friday before he was killed to ask if I was free on Monday afternoon. He said he had something personal to take care of earlier that morning."

Ed remembered Carol Smalley telling him the same thing.

Desmond continued, "You probably already know this, but my son, Greg, and his wife, Cheryl, are away on a lengthy cruise. I retired a while ago but agreed to come back to work until they return from their trip, but only for five or six hours a day. That's as much time as I was willing to commit at my age.

"When I was building the business, and even after, I often worked 12 to 14-hour days. When Greg and his sister, Wendy, were small, they were usually sleeping when I left in the morning and often when I came home at night. My wife, Mary Elizabeth, is a saint; she never complained.

"Now I arrive at 10:00 or 10:30 and leave no later than 5:00 to be home in time for cocktails with my wife. I told Noah to come by my office at 1:00."

"When he didn't show what did you think?"

"Reporters are busy. I thought maybe something else had come up that was more pressing and assumed he'd call to reschedule. Of course, I learned later what had happened to him."

"So run by me your schedule that day, if you don't mind. Again, it's just routine."

"Unfortunately, there's no one who can confirm my whereabouts before I arrived at work. My wife was visiting our granddaughter and her family in Washington state, and I was home alone in bed. I got up around 7:30, had coffee and breakfast , watched the news on TV and was in my office a little after 10:00. My secretary can attest to that. Would you like to speak with her?"

"That's not necessary," Ed responded. The man had no reason to lie.

"Thank you, Desmond, for speaking with me. I know you're a busy man so won't take up more of your time."

"I hope you find that young man's killer. If there's anything I or my family can do to help, let me know."

"I will. If you remember anything else, could you please give me a call?" Ed gave him his number.

"Of course. Good luck."

After taking a short break to get a glass of iced tea, Ed called the others on the list. He left messages for some. By the end of the day, he'd spoken with everyone and confirmed their alibis.

Like Desmond, they were either sleeping, getting ready for work, going for an early morning run or to a health club for a workout. Some had spouses who would vouch for them. Spousal affirmation was notoriously unreliable, but it didn't appear that anyone was lying. He decided not to check the types of cars they drove, and while he assumed several might be boat owners, none of them seemed to have anything to hide or a motive for killing the young reporter.

Ed called Robert Lessley. At first, the man said he was too busy to meet with him. Ed insisted, threatening to take legal steps if he refused to comply. After that, they agreed on a date and time. Ed wondered if he was stonewalling because, unlike the others, he had something to hide.

CHAPTER 36

After explaining her purpose for being at the library, Annie followed Holly Corcoran to a room with several computers.

She said, "Holly, supposedly the fire occurred in September 100 years ago. I don't know when the speakeasy Tony's Place opened, but I suspect it would have been at around the same time."

"I suggested Noah start with newspaper articles from *Silver Bay Times* using keywords like lake fire, rumrunners and Chimney Bluffs. He said he'd made good progress. You could add speakeasies or Tony's Place to the mix. This may be easier than you think but come and get me if you need help."

Annie typed the keywords into the search bar. Several minutes later, she was thrilled when she discovered not one, but two articles dating to the time of Noah's ancestor's death.

Silver Bay Times

July 11, 1925

BREAKING NEWS:
Suspicious Fire on Lake Ontario,
Local Brothers Missing

A boat fire on Lake Ontario last evening lit up the sky in communities near Chimney Bluffs and as far away as Kingston, Ontario, Canada. Although the cause of the fire is unknown, it is believed that Lighthouse Cove residents, Liam and Harry O'Connor, may have been among the casualties.

A missing person's report was filed early this morning by Harry's wife, Dorothy, when her husband and brother-in-law did not return from a fishing trip on the lake last night. They were expected home before midnight.

Heavy winds and waves cresting to ten feet have impeded further investigation.

We will keep you, our dear readers, informed as the case unfolds.

Silver Bay Times

July 14, 1925

UPDATE ON LAKE FIRE:
Investigation Commences

Rough seas and high winds over the past couple days have hindered the joint efforts of divers from the US and Canada to retrieve the bodies of those who perished on July 11 in a fire that occurred on Lake Ontario three miles offshore Chimney Bluffs. The investigation was able to commence early this morning after the winds died down.

Upon further questioning, Dorothy O'Connor admitted that her husband and his brother were bootleggers who, on the night of the fire, had arranged to meet up with rumrunners from Canada to purchase liquor to sell to local speakeasies.

Pregnant with the couple's first child, Mrs. O'Connor said that her husband had become increasingly fearful that at some point he and his brother would be apprehended and sent to jail and had planned to give notice that night that he was quitting the business to take a job as the manager of the Lighthouse Cove Hardware Store.

Just before noon, the divers retrieved an empty gasoline can and a Colt 1911 pistol

Silver Bay Times

July 14, 1925

from the bottom of the lake along with the charred remains of a Canadian schooner, *Black Duck*, and five bodies, whose descriptions from their loved ones helped to identify the Canadian victims, Simon Pierce, Eddy Watson, Sulley St. James, and the O'Connor brothers. Investigators believe the men were held at gunpoint while their killer doused the boat with gasoline and set it on fire and then tried to escape by jumping into the lake where they subsequently drowned.

Strong evidence implicates Etan Canersky, the owner of the schooner, as the perpetrator of the crime who may have fled the scene on O'Connor's boat, *Whyte Wytch*, along with the liquor and cash. An attempt to reach Canersky's wife, Phoebe, who resides in Kingston, Ontario, Canada with their young son, Frank, has been unsuccessful.

The funeral for the O'Connor brothers will be held at 10 a.m. on Friday morning at the Catholic Church in Lighthouse Cove, with internment for family members only at their cemetery plot on Lake Road. We will continue with updates when more information about this heinous crime is revealed.

CHAPTER 37

Annie pumped a fist. She was delighted by how quickly she'd found the information she was seeking. She opened her purse and retrieved a USB drive, copied the newspaper articles onto it and looked at her watch. It was time to head back to the museum.

Martha and Patrick Kelly, who volunteered in the gift shop, greeted her. She said she'd made progress at the library, then walked upstairs to Jason's office to tell him about it.

Back in her office, she turned on her computer, copied the articles from her USB drive to a file, and emailed them to Ed. At this point, there was nothing that appeared to be related to the murder investigation, but she'd promised to share with him whatever she found.

A short while later Martha rapped on her door, Elena Kane behind her.

"You have a guest," she said, smiled, and walked back to the gift shop.

"Welcome." Annie got up from behind her desk and the women hugged.

Elena said, "I feel like I've known you for much longer than a few days. I'm so happy we'll be able to spend the afternoon together."

"Me, too. My plan is to take you on a tour of the museum and then to lunch at one of our favorite cafés, Bistro Louise. It's casual but has great food and marvelous views, and their main server, Terri, is quite a character. I hope she's working today so you can meet her."

"Would you mind if we invited Suzanne? As I mentioned on Friday night, we haven't spent much time together lately, and I'd really like to see her."

"Great idea. She may be teaching a class, but I'll text her. If she can't do it today, we can plan for another time."

Annie sent the text, guided Elena through the building, and had just introduced her to Jason when her phone chimed with a response. Suzanne was unable to meet them for lunch but was looking forward to seeing them both soon.

"That's too bad; we certainly can coordinate schedules so the three of us can meet some other time, but Chris and I also discussed hosting a small dinner party for the six of us on our boat this summer. We'll look at dates, and I'll email you."

"We'd love that," Annie replied.

Back in her office, Annie handed Elena a packet of materials about the museum that included membership information and an invitation to the upcoming gala. Elena spent a few minutes reading through it.

"I'll purchase a family membership now. I'd also like to attend the gala, but I want to check with Chris to make sure he doesn't have a conflict. I don't think he'll be in court today. Give me a minute; I'll call him."

They spoke for a couple of minutes. Elena gave a thumbs up and ended the call.

"We're in."

She took a credit card out of her purse and handed it to Annie.

"Chris is a Civil War buff. I think he would be very interested in taking a tour of Macyville. Our summers are really busy, but maybe we could bring the kids some weekend during the fall, and I'd like to hear more about Fitzhugh House."

"There are guided tours at Macyville; the schedule is in the packet. Let me know when you plan to visit. If I'm able, I'll personally take you on the tour. Now, how about if we head to the bistro for lunch? I can drive if you'd prefer, or we can walk; it's only a few blocks, and we'll go right past Fitzhugh House. I'll tell you about it when we get there."

"It's such a beautiful day. Let's walk."

CHAPTER 38

They meandered through a neighborhood of historic homes with lake views. When they arrived at Fitzhugh House, Annie explained how the home had come to be in their possession.

"What a story. Is it as gorgeous inside as it is out?"

"It is, and there are spectacular gardens. Amanda Reynolds was quite the character, and we were friends for many years before she died in such a tragic way. When we have a little more time, I'll take you through it."

All the tables inside Bistro Louise were occupied, but there were a few on the deck with lake views and on the streetside patio that faced the bay.

"It might be a while before a table is available inside; air conditioning seems popular today. Instead, let's sit on the deck," Annie suggested. "It's noisier on the patio, and I like the lake view better."

"The deck is fine with me. I hate to waste days like this staying indoors."

Louise, who was behind the bakery counter, waved to them and said, "Go find a table. Terri will be with you soon to take your orders."

"Good. She's here," Annie said.

Within a couple minutes, the beautiful red-haired server, wearing the Bistro's signature red tee shirt and black leggings, walked over to them, nodded and said hello.

Annie introduced the two women. "This is my friend Elena Kane. She lives in Webster, and like you, is an artist; instead of ceramics, she works in mixed media."

Terri smiled, her green eyes shining. "Nice to meet you. I exhibit my pottery at a gallery here and participate in several artisans' festivals during weekends in the summer. I'd love to see your work. Where do you exhibit?"

"At a couple of galleries in Rochester, but I don't do festivals. My husband, Chris, and I have four children, and our weekends are busy."

Terri blushed, her eyes widened, then she quickly looked away.

Elena, curious about her reaction, asked, "Have you and Chris met?"

"His name sounds familiar. Let me think about it for a moment." She bit her lip. "Oh yes, of course. He's the Monroe County DA. After I graduated from high school about ten years ago, I moved to Rochester and worked as a server at an upscale restaurant near the courthouse. I think he was one of my regular customers. In fact, I'm sure of it. And I'm pretty certain my boyfriend, Dan, who's a detective with the Rochester city police, knows him."

"What restaurant was that?" Elena asked.

"Soleil."

"Hmm. Interesting."

Terri changed the subject. "Annie, it's such a small world. Dan was assigned to help Brad and the forensic techs in Rochester. Because of the Lighthouse Cove connection, he asked Brad if he knew me.

"Dan said Brad grinned and said he was a customer here and he knew me well. Dan was curious about his reaction and asked if we'd ever had a relationship. We're honest with each other; I admitted I'd had a crush on Brad, but nothing had happened between us. He was already head over heels for Felicia and wasn't remotely interested in me.

"Anyway, they apparently hit it off and talked about the four of us getting together for dinner sometime. To be perfectly honest, I'm not sure how I feel about that. I may still have a little bit of a crush on Brad."

She took their drink orders to give them time to peruse the menu.

CHAPTER 39

Elena was silent for a few seconds after the server walked away, then said, "Annie, what did you think about Terri's reaction when I mentioned Chris? Something seemed off about it. I was surprised when she said he'd been a customer at Soleil. I seem to remember him telling me he didn't like that restaurant, although it's possible he attended meetings there that he either didn't mention to me or maybe I just forgot. It has been, as she said, ten years."

"I wouldn't read anything into it, Elena. You heard how she rambled on about Brad, who, by the way, was never remotely interested in her. If it's true that Chris had some meetings at the restaurant when she was a server, she may have had an unrequited crush on your handsome husband, too, and was embarrassed about it when she realized you're his wife.

"She seems to have a thing for men in law enforcement. She also had a crush—unrequited again, by the way—on Brad's predecessor, Luke Callens, and we both heard her say she's dating a detective."

"Of course, you're probably right. Just out of curiosity, what else do you know about her?"

Annie smiled. "Remember, this is a very small village. Living here is a joy, but as typical in communities like ours, everyone knows everyone else's business. She's in her late twenties, was born and raised here, and as she said, lived in Rochester for a short time, probably no more than a year or two, after she graduated from high school."

"When she returned to Lighthouse Cove she started waitressing for Louise, and she's been here ever since. The café is only open each day until 3:00, and Terri doesn't work weekends, giving her time for her pottery."

"Is she always so chatty?"

"Depends on who the customer is. You should see her around Ed and Brad, especially when they're investigating a crime. She doesn't hesitate to give her opinion, and her questions are like the rapid fire of a BB gun."

She changed the subject. "Garrett said Chris is considering running for state attorney general."

"Yes, he is, but he hasn't made a decision yet."

"Garrett thinks the world of him and would support his candidacy in a heartbeat."

"He'd be a wonderful attorney general, Annie, but if he won, it would be a lot more work, and he's a bit concerned about the impact it would have on our family. He wouldn't be around much; he'd spend a lot of time in Albany. I want him to be happy, and the kids and I will support him with whatever decision he makes."

Their beverages arrived, and shortly after, their meals. After lunch, they walked back to the museum.

Elena hugged Annie. "It's been a lovely afternoon, and thank you so much for the tour and lunch; I've really enjoyed our time together. Chris and I are looking forward to seeing you and Ed at the gala. I'll be back in touch when we have some dates for our dinner party."

Annie smiled and waved to her new friend as she drove out of the parking lot.

That evening, while telling Ed about her delightful afternoon, she mentioned Terri's reaction when she figured out that Elena and Chris were married.

"At first, Elena seemed a bit disquieted, but after I assured her that Terri's always been a bit odd and to not read anything into it, she seemed fine."

"And you?"

"I admit Terri's reaction was a bit strange, Ed, but I don't want to read anything into it, either."

After dinner, she and Ed went into the study. He opened his computer and read the news articles she'd sent him about the fire on the lake.

Annie said, "I expect none of this has any relationship to your case, but I wanted to share what I found with you anyway. I'm not going to send Noah's parents the newspaper articles just yet. I'm curious about whether this Canersky person was ever apprehended."

CHAPTER 40

During the debriefing with Carrie the next morning, Ed and Brad admitted that the investigation was stalled. Carrie thought it might be time to send a press release to local media outlets asking readers to contact her with tips that would help solve the crime.

After the meeting ended, Brad and Mia headed out to investigate a robbery at the local convenience store, and Ed drove home. Until his appointment the next day at the chamber of commerce, there was nothing more he could do. He decided to spend the rest of the day cleaning the garage.

By late afternoon, in response to the release, Carrie had received a few calls, but the leads went nowhere. One was from a charter boat captain who said he saw a yacht, *Treasure of the Seas*, with a Toronto port of call near Chimney Bluffs the morning of Noah's death. Several people on it waved as they passed. Carrie called Customs. The yacht belonged to the CEO of Scotiabank—there was no reason to contact him.

A couple reported they had seen a young man hiking the trail at the Bluffs at 7:30 that morning. Noah was probably already dead by that time, and the description didn't match.

A young woman said she and her boyfriend had spent the night on his boat and reported seeing a young man in a yellow kayak near Chimney Bluffs early that morning and wondered if he was the victim, but Carrie assured her that the investigators had spoken with the man; he was very much alive.

Brad and Mia returned from the convenience store. Cameras had recorded the robber escaping in a car with a clear view of the license plate, and they apprehended him at his home in Lyons. Carrie gave him an update about responses to the press release and then called Ed.

"Thanks, Carrie, but remember you just released it. You may still get some responses."

"I know. Hope everything goes well with your interview tomorrow. I'll be here if you need me."

"Thanks. Have a good evening."

"You, too."

CHAPTER 41

Early the next morning, before Ed left for his interview with Robert Lessley, his phone rang.

"Hi, Carrie. What's up?"

"Sorry it's taken me so long, but I finally got around to doing a background check on Belinda Corey. I'm pretty sure she didn't kill Noah.

"She doesn't own a boat, nor does it appear she recently rented one. She lives in a studio apartment in the city and drives a pre-owned white Subaru Forester. I didn't find any irregular financial expenditures—no large payments to anyone—so it's unlikely she hired a hitter.

"I have no idea what type of relationship she has with her parents; that information obviously wouldn't appear in a background check, but I learned that they recently divorced. Her mother is an art critic who moved to Spain with an artist she met at a conference in France last year, and her father works at an ad agency in Rochester.

"She's the youngest of five and the only girl. Her brothers are scattered around the country. Oh, and one of her grandmothers died several weeks ago. There was an obit in the Rochester paper.

"She posted on social media about her grandmother's death and also that she recently euthanized her dog, Victor, an older Corgi she adopted from a no-kill rescue shelter shortly after she graduated from college."

Ed responded, "The young woman certainly has had a lot of upheaval in her life; maybe telling Eric she was Noah's fiancée was a grab for sympathy and attention. I hope she's getting some professional help; sounds like she needs it.

"I'll take her off my list as a suspect. Good news for Belinda, but I'm not sure where to go next."

"Be patient, Ed. This case will be solved. They almost always are."

Ed had a thought and called Eric Klein. "Eric, I asked our police chief to run a background check on Belinda Corey; she's in the clear. I can't reveal the details, but she has experienced quite a bit of trauma and loss recently. She needs support and probably some professional help, if she's not getting it already. Anything you can do to help?"

"Of course, and thanks for letting me know. I'll reach out to her. We exchanged phone numbers after we spoke at the grocery store. I'm sure Lily won't object if I invite her for dinner some night; maybe we can get her to open up. I have a friend who teaches in the psychology department who I expect can refer her to a good therapist if it comes to that."

"Thanks, Eric."

"You have such empathy, Ed. It's one of the things I like about you, and I know it's one of the qualities that George admired and made you such close friends. I'll see what I can do and call you with an update."

CHAPTER 42

Traffic was light, and Ed arrived at the chamber of commerce office several minutes early for his 10:30 meeting with Robert Lessley. He presented his ID to the receptionist in the lobby and informed her that he had an appointment with the chamber executive.

She placed a call, and within a couple minutes, a thirty-something, brown-skinned woman with curly dark hair cropped short, large brown eyes and French-manicured nails appeared. She was wearing a black skirt suit with black three-inch heels, diamond studs in her ears and a slim gold bracelet around her right wrist.

"Good morning, I'm Naomi Ellison, Bob's administrative assistant. Please follow me."

She ushered him onto an elevator that stopped on the fifth floor. Her desk sat in an anteroom where colorful photos of Rochester landmarks adorned the walls and a large potted Ficus tree sat in a light-filled corner. She walked past her desk, rapped on a closed door, announced Ed's arrival and opened it before her boss could respond.

Lessley looked startled. He was standing behind his desk holding a pill bottle in each hand. He hastily placed them in a side drawer, and, taking a key from a ring, locked it. Then he leaned over and shook Ed's hand.

In his late 50s and just under six feet tall with a stocky build, short brown hair turning gray, and warm brown eyes, he was wearing a dark blue suit with a light blue shirt, red and blue striped rep tie and well-polished black oxford shoes. A wide gold wedding band and a chrome-faced watch with a black leather strap were his only jewelry.

Ed quickly glanced around the room. Wall-hung black and white photos of office buildings and shopping centers hung in strategic spots, with Lessley standing alongside city and state dignitaries at ribbon cuttings.

Small photos of what appeared to be friends and family had been placed on the credenza behind his desk, including one with him standing on the swim platform of a motorboat with his arm around a smiling dark-haired woman with large, dark eyes.

He motioned for Ed to sit in one of two leather swivel chairs in front of the desk. He sat next to him in the other, then turned toward him.

"Okay if I call you Ed? You can call me Bob." He glanced at his watch and jiggled his right leg. He seemed nervous.

Hoping to put the man at ease he said, "I noticed the photos, very nice. Is the woman with you on the boat your wife?"

He smiled. "She is. Her name is Amira. We've been married for 35 years, and she's the love of my life."

"Do you spend much time on the boat?"

"Not as much as we'd like to. Busy lives, you know."

"Ever sail to Chimney Bluffs?"

"Where your young reporter was murdered? Can't say we have. It's a long trip; we mainly sail around Irondequoit Bay or when we go out to the lake, no farther than Pultneyville for dinner at a restaurant there that has a few boat docks and outdoor seating.

Ed nodded. "Bob, Carol Smalley, the editor of the *Rochester Daily News* said you travel to Mexico with a group of other chamber executives from our region for business. Been there lately?"

"Actually, no. The last visit was in April. We went to Juarez, across the border from El Paso; there's a furniture manufacturer we've been negotiating with."

He glanced at his watch. "Ed, I appreciate that you're trying to put me at ease with the small talk, but I'm quite used to being interviewed, and I have another meeting in half-an-hour. I know you want to speak with me about the murder of Noah Pierce, but there's nothing I can tell you. We'd never met. He called to schedule an appointment to interview me, but we couldn't coordinate schedules."

"This is just pro forma, Bob, but I have to ask your whereabouts early on the morning Noah Pierce was killed." He provided the date.

He shrugged and started jiggling his right foot. "I expect I was here all day; that's usually where I am during the week."

"The sign on the front door says the office opens at 8:00. Is there someone who can verify that you were here
, perhaps your administrative assistant?"

Lessley's foot jiggled a little faster. "Well, let's see. Oh yes, I forgot. I came in around 10:30 that day."

"And where were you before then?"

"It's really none of your business, and it has nothing to do with the murder."

"Then I'm not sure why you're not being forthcoming."

"I had some appointments. Again, nothing to do with the murder."

Lessley's phone buzzed.

He answered it, sighed and said impatiently, "No, don't do that. I have to sign for it. Tell him I'll be right down."

"Excuse me a minute. My assistant has informed me that a package I've been expecting has arrived. I need to sign for it; the courier is downstairs in the lobby. It won't take long."

CHAPTER 43

He returned with a large envelope, glanced at Ed, then hurriedly walked over to a coat closet and placed it on a shelf above the hanging garments.

"My apologies; there shouldn't be any more interruptions," he said.

"Then let me get to the point. We are aware that Peyton Stewart is your nephew. What can you tell me about him?"

"He went to jail because he got caught selling drugs. Do you think he killed your reporter?" His leg started jiggling again. He glanced at the closet where he'd placed the envelope and looked at his watch.

"We were never close. He's always been willful and unruly, despite his parents' attempts to discipline him. I'm sorry he hasn't been able to get his life together; fortunately, it appears my sister's constituents aren't holding her responsible for her son's crime. She still has a high approval rating.

"I can't imagine he's your killer; he's in jail. He's not wealthy enough to have ordered a hit. His accounts were frozen, and his parents would never be party to something like that.

"Why would he want to, anyway, unless your reporter was the one who outed him? In that case, I suppose it's also possible that my nephew's supplier had him killed, but since Peyton refused to reveal his identity and no one seems to have a clue about who he is, that would be really hard to prove, wouldn't it?"

He glanced at his watch again. "Ed, I'm sorry I couldn't help you, but I really need to get to that meeting."

Ed handed him a card. "I appreciate your time. If you can think of anything, please call. I can see myself out."

CHAPTER 44

Ed had just pulled into his driveway when his phone pinged with a text from Carrie: *"Call me when you get a chance."*

Minutes later, he called her from his study.

"Hi, Carrie. You beat me to it. I was going to call you. What's up?"

She said, "Just touching base. I assume you've finished your interview with Lessley. How did it go?"

"There's something squirrely about the man, Carrie."

He informed her about Lessley's behavior: his nervousness and refusal to answer straightforward questions, the pill bottles, the package, and the conversation about Peyton.

"There's a photo of him and his wife on their boat, but he says he's never sailed to Chimney Bluffs. He admitted to trips to Mexico for business, but he hasn't been there since April. That would be easy enough to prove."

"What about his alibi?"

"He was somewhat vague. He said he had appointments first thing in the morning, but refused to tell me what they were, and after that was in his office for the rest of the day. He wasn't exactly hostile, but he put up a wall that he clearly was not going to let me penetrate.

"When I asked about his nephew, he said Peyton couldn't have killed Noah; he's in jail and didn't have the money to hire a hit, which makes sense.

"He speculated that Noah might have been the one who outed his nephew, and in that case, perhaps his nephew's supplier had him killed. But since Peyton wouldn't identify him and no one seems to know who he is, it would be hard to prove. Given his demeanor when he said it, I felt as though he were baiting me.

"I don't know if he was Peyton's supplier or even if he killed Noah, but he's definitely hiding something. I plan to schedule another interview."

Carrie said, "Perhaps you should take Brad with you next time."

"I agree. I'll let you know when I schedule it."

Ed wrote a report and placed a call to Lessley, who was out of the office for meetings. He left a message indicating he had some follow-up questions.

He needed a break. He prepared a sandwich, placed it and a bottle of water in a backpack along with a plastic bag of kibbles and a canteen for Gretchen, and lifted her into his SUV. Two miles west on Lake Road he turned right into the parking lot at Beechwood State Park, the site of a German prisoner of war camp during WWII, that was purchased years later by the state department of parks and recreation.

He sat at a picnic table in the woods, dropping tiny kibbles for Gretchen who stared at him, licking her lips, as he ate. After, they walked along a path that led to a rocky bluff with spectacular views of the lake where he could see the Oswego skyline, thirty miles away.

He felt better. His head had cleared, and he trusted that the case would eventually be solved, even if Robert Lessley wasn't Noah's killer. But there was still something that unsettled him.

CHAPTER 45

Ed called the chamber of commerce again the next morning and this time asked to speak with Naomi Ellison, who said that Lessley had received his message but had been too busy to call him back and was currently unavailable.

He phoned Carrie. "He's blowing me off, and I'm losing patience. Do you remember Chris Bayley?"

"Of course I do; he's the FBI agent who worked behind the scenes with you and Annie on your last case."

"That's right. I think it's time for me to call and ask him to do a little digging. I assume his agency is able to interface with other federal intelligence agencies. Lessley's up to something, but at this point I have no idea what it is."

"Good idea."

"I'll get back to you as soon as I learn anything, but it probably won't be until the beginning of the week. Annie and I are heading out later this afternoon for a mini vacation before Noah's funeral. There's not much I can do until then anyway. Would you mind checking the make and model of his car?"

"I'll ask Mia to run it and text you when I have the information. I'm glad you and Annie are taking some time for yourselves, Ed. You've been working hard on this case and deserve a break. Are you going to spend the entire time in Gananoque? We've never been there, but I hear it's charming."

"It is. We've been there before, but tonight we're staying in Sackets Harbor. We'll spend tomorrow morning in Clayton before heading to Canada. Summers are usually crazy busy for Annie, but she has enough staff and docents now to run the museum when she's away. She needs a break, too."

With a little time to spare before Annie got home, Ed called the FBI agent, who worked at both the Rochester and Buffalo offices, and sometimes from his home.

"Good morning. This is Chris Bayley."

"Hi, Chris, it's Ed DeCleryk."

"Hi, Ed. It's been a long time. How can I help you?"

Ed apprised him of the murder investigation and his interview with Robert Lessley.

"Can you see what he's up to? We know he travels to Mexico for business; he says the last time was in Juarez in April. I wonder if there have been other trips there that aren't business-related, and if he's on any federal agencies' radar."

"Certainly. It might take me a while. I'll get back to you as soon as I learn anything."

"That's no problem. Annie and I will be away for a few days; we'll be back on Saturday evening. Thanks, Chris."

Shortly after they ended the call, Ed's phone rang. Robert Lessley apologized for the delay in returning Ed's calls. He'd been unusually busy, but could meet with him on Monday at 10:00 a.m. This time he was cordial but sounded tired.

Ed called Carrie. She said Brad would pick Ed up at 9:00 that day to give them plenty of time to get to the chamber of commerce office before the meeting.

CHAPTER 46

Annie had just finished giving a tour to a group of seniors from Canandaigua. A docent had called and said he wouldn't be in that day on account of a family emergency. She glanced at her watch.

She had plenty of time to go to the library to continue her research and be home by mid-afternoon. The drive to Sackets Harbor took slightly more than two hours; their dinner reservation wasn't until 7:30. She grabbed a couple of granola bars from her desk, gobbled them down, then headed out.

Beginning where she'd previously left off, she quickly discovered another news article with information about Etan Canersky that, this time, included a photo.

Silver Bay Times

August 1, 1925

BREAKING NEWS
Manhunt Ensues

Federal, state and local law enforcement agencies have undertaken a massive manhunt for Canadian rumrunner Etan Canersky who, as previously reported, is being sought as the primary suspect in the deaths of several Canadian rumrunners and two of our residents, Liam and Harry O'Connor. We have recently learned that the culprit is also wanted in Kingston, Ontario for assault and arson and in Belleville, Ontario for murder.

Authorities speculate that the villain, who fled to safety on Liam O'Connor's shadow boat, *Whyte Wytch*, is hiding with his wife and child here in Wayne County. The boat remains missing and is believed to have been destroyed.

Canersky, whose photo was provided to us by law enforcement officials in Canada, is 5'6", 145 pounds, with short, slicked-back blond hair, pale blue eyes and a small scar above his upper lip. If you see this man, contact the Lighthouse Cove police or federal authorities with information, but do not approach him. He may be armed and dangerous. All reports will be kept confidential.

CHAPTER 47

Ed arrived home after walking Gretchen to find Annie lugging a suitcase down the steps from their bedroom.

"Annie, what are you doing? Why didn't you wait for me to carry that?" He started to take it from her.

"It's not all that heavy, Ed; we're just taking a short trip. I figured while you were walking Gretchen, I'd start loading the car."

"How did the research go at the library?"

"I discovered another newspaper article with a photo of Etan Canersky. I emailed it to you with an attachment."

He opened the email on his phone and read it. "Fascinating. You're making really good progress."

They dropped Gretchen off at the sitter's, then headed to Sackets Harbor. The village, situated along the eastern end of Lake Ontario, was the site of a shipyard built to support the War of 1812, and where two decisive battles had been held during that war.

On the way, Ed described his interview with Robert Lessley and told her about his conversation with Chris Bayley. He hoped that by the time they returned home, the agent would have information for him.

Within minutes after checking into the Augustus Sacket Inn, the couple was escorted to a spacious room with a view of the harbor, a fireplace, an enormous four-poster bed and a small seating area. They unpacked their clothing, changed into dressy-casual attire, and went down to the lobby bar for happy hour. They had just started mingling with some of the other guests, when Ed's phone pinged with a message from Carrie.

He excused himself and walked outside to read it: "*Lessley and his wife co-own a Mini Cooper convertible, white and tan, and a two-year-old Mazda CX-50, dark navy blue.*"

He texted back: "*Thanks, it wasn't quite dawn when the cameras caught someone picking Noah up the day he died. I suppose navy could look black under the right circumstances.*"

Ed had made a reservation at the Old Stone Tavern, built as an inn and pub shortly after the War of 1812 ended. They were seated outside on a courtyard patio surrounded by potted Japanese maples, beds filled with colorful summer perennials, and lighted tiki torches. Ed mentioned the text, and he and Annie made a joint decision to spend the rest of the evening not talking about work.

The server took their drink orders, a scotch for Ed and Sauvignon Blanc for Annie, and while they waited for their beverages, they perused the menu and listened to the smooth sounds of a jazz combo that was performing on a small stage adjacent to the bar.

A couple hours later, having enjoyed their meals and the music, and too full for dessert, they walked back to the inn where they read for a while and, exhausted from the long day, fell quickly asleep.

CHAPTER 48

Checking out of the inn after breakfast the next morning, they headed for Clayton, a charming New York waterside town located in the Thousand Islands across the St. Lawrence River from Gananoque.

They toured an antique boat museum, which, to Annie's delight, included a shadow boat and schooner from rumrunning days, and meandered through galleries and boutiques. They stopped at a gift shop where Ed purchased boxes of home-made fudge for Carrie, Brad and Barb, and Annie bought coffee mugs, designed by a local potter, for Eve and Suzanne.

Dresses in a window display at a women's boutique caught Annie's eye, just as Ed's phone rang. The caller was Chris Bayley. He walked over to the curb, sat on a bench and picked up.

"Hi, Ed. It's Chris. I have information for you."

Annie touched Ed on the shoulder and motioned that she was going to go inside the boutique. He nodded.

"Hi, Chris."

"I can verify Lessley's trips to Mexico for business, and he was telling you the truth when he said the last one was in April.

"But I also learned that Lessley flies to San Miguel de Allende every couple weeks or so for long weekends. He apparently has accrued a lot of vacation time.

"What's interesting is that he never checks any luggage, just a carry-on. When he gets there he's a ghost. As foolish as it may be, he must bring a lot of cash with him; there are no credit card charges. Where he stays is anyone's guess; there's no evidence he books a hotel room.

"His most recent trip was the weekend before your victim was killed. He left on a Thursday and returned late on Sunday night. Because of the frequency of trips, he's on customs' radar, but they've never found a reason to detain him when he goes through security."

"He's married. Does his wife ever accompany him?"

"No, he travels solo."

"I wonder what excuses he makes to her for being gone so many weekends. When did he start traveling there?"

"A few months ago."

"Around the same time, his nephew was arrested. Is there much of a drug trade in San Miguel?"

"Not as much as in other parts of Mexico. The Federales have a large presence, but the cartels are making inroads, although for now they are leaving tourist areas alone. If he's smuggling drugs, someone else is bringing them into the country."

"Noah wanted to be an investigative reporter. Maybe after Peyton Stewart was arrested, he did some digging. If he discovered that Lessley was involved...."

"And Lessley learned about it, he could have had him killed."

"Correct. We know he owns a boat, and he also drives a late model Mazda SUV. It's navy, but it was just before dawn when the camera outside Noah's apartment recorded a black SUV picking him up. Navy could look black in a certain light."

"What's next?"

"Another meeting, this time an interrogation rather than an interview. Brad Washington will be accompanying me. If we don't get the answers we're seeking, I'll put some pressure on him; he might be more forthcoming if he knows our next stop will be a visit to his wife. Thanks, Chris. I appreciate your help."

"You're very welcome. Keep me posted."

"I will."

He placed his phone back in his pocket just as Annie emerged from the boutique, carrying a bag with a dress and a pair of sandals. They walked to a riverfront café. During lunch, she showed him her new clothing, and he told her about his conversation with Chris Bayley.

CHAPTER 49

They drove over the Thousand Islands Bridge, and after going through customs, arrived at the Inn at Gananoque. A valet unloaded their suitcases and parked their car.

They checked in and made a reservation for dinner at 7:30 at the inn's upscale restaurant, Harborview. Their spacious room had a river view, king-sized bed covered with a jewel-toned comforter, two matching wing chairs and a fireplace. After unpacking, they took a walk through the quaint, historic part of town, then went back to their room to shower and change for dinner.

Tall windows framed by billowing white curtains provided stunning river views; a large, ornately carved oak fireplace dominated a wall at one end of the restaurant. Tables set with ivory cloths and rose-colored damask napkins, gold-rimmed ivory dishes, etched crystal wine and beverage goblets, silver flatware, and centerpieces of square glass vases filled with colorful dahlias and zinnias gleamed under the lights of two large prismed crystal chandeliers.

Ed ordered a dry martini, up, and Annie a glass of dry Rosé from an Ontario Province winery. A few minutes later, their server handed them menus, recited the daily specials, and after serving their drinks, took their orders—entrees featuring locally sourced ingredients. While waiting for their salads, the couple sipped their drinks and helped themselves to freshly baked rolls accompanied by strawberry butter.

After dinner, they wandered outside to the candlelit patio for coffee and dessert, then to their room where a bouquet of colorful summer blooms—daisies, lilies, irises and Black-eyed Susans—had been placed on a dresser for Annie with a card signed with a heart from Ed.

Delighted, she kissed him. "You certainly know how to treat a girl. What's the occasion?"

"Do I need one to show you how much I love you?"

Annie raised an eyebrow, "No, but am I correct in assuming you have an ulterior motive? Perhaps the flowers are a prelude to something, should I say, more intimate?"

Ed grinned, drew his wife to him and kissed her back. "Well, you may be right about that. Interested?"

"You betcha."

The couple slept soundly that night, snuggled in each other's arms.

The next morning, they walked a block to board a boat for a tour of several of the unique islands, and spent the afternoon at the inn's spa before having an early dinner at the casual restaurant, The Wheelhouse, where they ate barbecue and listened to the sounds of a country western band.

They headed up to their room, set the alarm, and soon after, exhausted, fell asleep. The funeral started at 10 a.m. the next morning, and they wanted to make sure they were awake early enough to get to the church to find seats. They expected the sanctuary would be filled with mourners; for latecomers, standing room only.

CHAPTER 50

The service was held at the local Presbyterian church, a grand stone edifice with a tall, regal spire that was built in 1870 after the original small wooden structure dating back to the 1840s became too small for the expanding congregation. It sat back from the road, surrounded by colorful, lush gardens, stands of tall deciduous trees, and at the far end, a cemetery with a river view.

Inside, sunlight streamed through vivid stained-glass windows into the large, peaceful sanctuary painted cream and robin's egg blue, with gleaming burnished wooden pews on either side of a center aisle. The first two rows had been reserved for family members, the closed casket between them in front of the pulpit. Multiple floral arrangements in stately green funereal vases clustered nearby, the smell of spicy carnations, clove-scented roses, and gardenias redolent of coconut and peach permeating the air.

The DeCleryks were greeted by two young ushers who led them to pews set aside for non-family members. Just as they were about to sit, Ed noticed Carol Smalley walking down the aisle with Noah's friends from work, Ajani and Melissa. She stopped at their pew, smiled, greeted Ed and introduced herself to Annie.

"Hello, I'm Carol Smalley and these are two of our reporters, Ajani Amibola and Melissa Duncan. You must be Annie."

"How nice to meet you," Annie said. "Ed mentioned how helpful you've been with his investigation."

They stood and talked for a few minutes, then Melissa said, "Mr. DeCleryk, maybe I shouldn't be bringing this up now, but Belinda Corey called me a few days after Noah died and asked for funeral details. Noah's parents don't have a landline; she wasn't able to find cell phone numbers or other contact information for them online, and there was no specific information about it in his obituary. She said she wanted to pay her respects.

"I said I didn't know the date, but that I'd heard the funeral would be private—family members only. I hated to lie, but it was the only thing I could think of to make sure she didn't attend."

Ed smiled. "Perfect response, Melissa. Noah's family certainly doesn't need a drama queen creating a scene here today."

The DeCleryks scooted toward the center of the pew and invited Carol and the reporters to join them. Minutes later, every seat in the church was taken in the main sanctuary and on the balcony, with, as they expected, standing room only at the back of the church for latecomers.

The service was brief with psalms, hymns, and reminiscences about Noah from some of his friends. Julie Pierce sobbed into a handkerchief, her husband's arm around her, tears dripping down his cheeks. Toward the end of the service, they walked to the podium to speak but were so overcome with emotion that they couldn't continue.

Their daughter stood, and taking deep, steadying breaths, talked about her relationship with her brother, a kind, quiet man who cared deeply for his family and died too soon.

The service ended. Some of Noah's college friends and his brother-in-law served as pallbearers. White gloved, they solemnly lifted the casket and carried it to the cemetery, followed by a procession of mourners.

At the gravesite, the minister recited the 23rd psalm and led the group in the hymn, *How Great Thou Art*. Family members placed long-stemmed white roses on the casket before it was lowered into the ground, then everyone walked back to the church for a luncheon reception in the social hall.

CHAPTER 51

Annie lingered, telling Ed to go ahead without her. She had struck out when she attempted to find the cemetery where the O'Connor brothers had been buried. Most family plots near Lighthouse Cove were on private land, but she hoped she would be more successful in locating Simon Pierce's grave.

She wandered along, looking at headstones, curious about what stories the dead would tell. Then she found it: *Simon Pierce, June 6, 1900–September 11, 1925, Beloved Husband and Father, Lost at Sea But Never Forgotten.*

Next to his headstone was that of his wife Helen, who it appeared, had never remarried and died a decade later. Annie wondered about the cause of death, given her age. During the first half of the 20th century, many young people perished from contagious diseases.

Their son, Simon Pierce Jr. who had been an infant when his father was killed, lived until he was 75. Nearby were headstones engraved with the names of other Pierce family members, spanning generations.

Sam and Julie Pierce were standing near the buffet table when Annie returned to the social hall. She walked over to them, introduced herself, and they spoke quietly for a few minutes. She spied Ed sitting at a table in the back of the room with Carol Smalley, the two young reporters and some friends of the Pierce family.

She quietly told him about finding Simon Pierce's grave; he said he'd spoken with Julie and Sam's siblings and some nieces and nephews. No one had information that would help to solve the crime.

A parishioner walked over to their table and directed them to the buffet. After they finished eating, the couple said goodbye to the Pierces, and Ed promised that either he or Brad would call them with updates about the investigation.

Back in Lighthouse Cove, they collected Gretchen from the pet-sitter and unpacked the suitcase, planning to get takeout from the Brewery for dinner. Annie was outside in the yard with Gretchen when Ed's phone rang. It was Brad. They chatted for a while about the funeral, then he asked if Ed and Annie wanted to join him and Felicia at La Estrellita for dinner that evening.

"I know it's spur of the moment, but I figured you might not want to cook tonight. We can make it early."

"Give me a minute. Annie's outside. I'll ask her."

A minute later he said, "We're in, but Annie's wondering if you would be okay with including Suzanne and Garrett."

"That's a great idea, Ed. Felicia is out running errands, but I can't imagine she'd have a problem with it. Go ahead and call them."

Several hours later, the three couples gathered on the covered patio—sparkling orange, green and white fairy lights dancing on the latticed roof above them—to enjoy delicious Mexican cuisine and listen to the festive sounds of a mariachi band.

Later, the couple agreed that despite the sadness of attending Noah's funeral, it had been a lovely weekend indeed.

CHAPTER 52

Brad picked Ed up at 9:00 on Monday morning, and the two investigators headed to the chamber office for the meeting with Robert Lessley. They had just entered the highway when Brad asked, "Do you have a police scanner?"

"I do, but half the time it's turned off. Why?"

"The bathhouse and snack bar at the municipal beach were vandalized last night, and the perps also set a couple of trash cans on fire."

"I didn't have the scanner on, but now that you mention it, I did hear sirens. Anyone injured?"

"No, some neighbors reported it; fortunately the fires were extinguished before spreading."

"Any idea who did it?"

"Not yet. Mia and I will be working the case. We think it might be a group of kids; we found some marijuana joints and beer cans on the beach, but at this point it's anybody's guess whether they were local or visitors. As soon as we get back I'll start working on it."

When they arrived at the chamber of commerce office, Naomi Ellison was waiting for them. Ed introduced Brad and said he'd be sitting in on the interview. She led them to a small conference room where a plate of donuts and a coffee service had been placed on a small credenza.

"He'll be a minute; he's finishing up a call," she said. "Help yourselves to the goodies."

They had just sat down with glazed donuts and cups of coffee when Lessley entered the room. Naomi had alerted him that Ed was accompanied by another investigator; he walked over to Brad, introduced himself, and the two men shook hands.

For a few minutes, they exchanged pleasantries, then Ed dispensed with small talk.

"I'm going to be honest with you, Bob; you weren't very forthcoming the first time we met. If you weren't involved in Noah Pierce's death, you need to tell us why you evaded answering my questions so I can take you off my suspect list."

Lessley sighed. "I'm not stupid, Ed. The interview didn't go well, and I accept responsibility for that. I admit I was nervous, which is unlike me, but it's not what you think."

"Over the weekend, I realized that my vague responses and lack of cooperation may have led you to believe I killed Noah Pierce. I think I told you that he and I never met. I wasn't blowing him off; I had too much on my plate to schedule a meeting. I assure you I've never used illegal substances or purchased or supplied them to anyone. I had nothing to do with his death.

"I completely understand why my behavior raised some red flags. I admit I didn't want to speak with you again, but when you called the third time, I decided it was time for candor. I understand you'll need to report what I say to your police chief, but I'd appreciate your not sharing it with anyone else. My staff doesn't even know what I'm about to tell you."

"Fair enough. Let's start from scratch. Where were you the morning Noah was killed?"

"I had a doctor's appointment at 8:00. After that, I drove home for a Zoom meeting with my wife, our son, Ethan, and daughter-in-law, Maria. They are oncologists who, after completing residencies at Anderson Cancer Center in Texas, relocated to San Miguel where Maria's family lives.

"They have been treating Amira for a rare form of blood cancer. An experimental treatment there hasn't been approved in the states but has shown promise in Mexico, with many patients experiencing long-term remission.

"The package you saw me placing in my closet contained her latest X-rays, blood test results, an extensive treatment plan and a progress report. I was impatient for you to leave so I could read them before I went to the meeting. If you want to stop by my house later today, I'll show you the documents, but I won't let you make copies; that's personal information that has no bearing on your investigation.

"I travel to San Miguel as often as I can to be with my wife. I've accrued a lot of vacation time and tell my staff I'm using up some of it over the summer for long weekends. I would have taken an early retirement, but honestly, I still need to work. While medical treatment in Mexico is less expensive, it's still fairly costly and our insurance here will not cover it.

"We have three children, and my wife was a stay-at-home mom. It was a joint decision. I make a good living and we've managed to save, but our kids are all college-educated, and we've paid for two of their weddings. If I stopped working now, we'd blow through our savings accounts pretty quickly."

"I wish you had been more forthcoming during the first interview, Bob; then we could have moved on. I'm sorry to hear about your wife," Ed said.

"I have one more question: You were holding two bottles of pills when I entered your office the first time. If you had nothing to hide, why did you lock them in your drawer?

"I adore my wife, and we've had a long and happy marriage. That I could lose her is causing me immeasurable anguish. I've been having panic attacks, and my blood pressure has soared. As I said, I had a doctor's appointment that morning. She prescribed medicine for both my anxiety and blood pressure issues. I picked up the prescriptions on my way to work. I've just started seeing a therapist.

"Naomi isn't great with boundaries, and I know at times when I'm out of the office she'll go through the top drawer of my desk if she needs a pencil, tablet or a paper clip rather than visiting the supply closet.

"I'm relatively certain she wouldn't go into any of my other desk drawers without my permission, but I locked the bottles in a side drawer as a safeguard. I believe I mentioned I had another meeting to go to afterward. I wanted to make sure the pills were secure until I returned and could take them home with me that night.

"I'm not ready to talk with my staff about my wife's condition or my own issues. I plan on telling them soon; I'm going to need their support."

"Bob, it's not necessary for us to see your wife's personal information, but I would like confirmation from your doctor that you had an appointment the morning of Noah Pierce's death."

"I have no problem with that. I'll email you with her name and phone number once I sign the permission slips."

Brad had been sitting quietly, arms crossed during the interview. Now, angry, he spoke.

"I'm sorry for what you are experiencing, too, but you do realize that if you had been honest with Ed the first time, we wouldn't be having this conversation today? We have enough on our plates with normal police business and trying to find Noah Pierce's killer without wasting our time."

Lessley sighed. "Nothing excuses the way I acted; I feel terrible that a promising young reporter is dead. I can't imagine what that's been like for his family. I hope you can understand that I was in a particularly bad emotional state when Ed interviewed me."

Brad glared at the chamber president and didn't respond.

Ed said, "I truly hope things work out for you and that your wife recovers. My wife and I have been happily married for more than 40 years, and I know I'd be a basket case if she were fighting a terminal illness."

Brad drove back to Lighthouse Cove while Ed texted Carrie and Chris Bayley with updates.

When he finished, he said, "Brad, I understand you're angry, but you need to let this go."

"I am angry, Ed. This ended up being a gross waste of time. I could have spent the morning working on that fire at the beach instead of playing footsie with Lessley, and you could have spent the time looking for other suspects."

"You're right. But consider it from Lessley's perspective. He was apprehensive about what the test results would reveal and is scared he's going to lose his wife. As he admitted, I caught him on a particularly bad day. I feel bad for the guy. Have a little empathy."

Brad looked contrite and sighed. "Okay, maybe I overreacted. A couple of hours away from the station won't make that much of a difference. Now I feel bad that I landed so hard on him. I should have kept my mouth shut."

"Don't beat yourself up about it; just remember for the next time."

CHAPTER 53

Ed had plans to meet some friends, all former Navy SEALs, for lunch that day. As soon as he got home, he changed out of business attire to shorts and a golf shirt and headed to Phillips House, a restaurant that stood high on a hill overlooking acres of apple orchards with a view of the lake in the distance.

It was another beautiful day, with the sun beating down in a clear blue sky, and a light, cooling breeze. His friends were sitting at a table on the deck when he arrived.

The men ordered, and while waiting for their meals, chatted amiably. Ed gave a brief report about the status of the murder investigation; then one of the group, Larry Mandel, asked Ed how Annie was doing.

"Funny you should ask," he responded, and explained about the discovery of the speakeasy and her research at the library to find out what happened to Noah Pierce's ancestor.

"She'd love to speak with someone who was alive then but realizes it's highly unlikely given that it's been more than a century since the law was passed."

Larry responded, "My uncle, Max Green, was a young boy during the last years of Prohibition. He may be willing to speak with her. He's 98 and living in a continuing care facility in

Newark, but he grew up near Lighthouse Cove. His body is frail, but his mind is still very sharp. Our family learned recently that his father ran a speakeasy.

"He was somewhat embarrassed about it, but we assured him it was nothing to be ashamed of. His father had a family to support, and before Prohibition, he'd been the proprietor of a lucrative bar and restaurant. Thanks to the Temperance Society, most of his income quickly dried up.

"Give me a minute; I'll call him. He doesn't use a cell phone, just a landline. If he doesn't pick up, I'll leave a message."

Larry's uncle answered after several rings, apologizing for the delay. He used a cane and sometimes a walker to get around which slowed him down. He agreed to speak with Annie, and asked Larry to have her call to arrange a meeting.

CHAPTER 54

While Ed was at lunch, Annie was waiting at the museum for the truck from Kane Global Transport.

Three burly men arrived at 12:30. Forty-five minutes later, with the speakeasy items stored safely, she thanked them for helping her and handed them chilled bottles of water and family seasonal passes for admission to the museum and Macyville.

Annie called Elena to thank her for helping to set things up; when she didn't answer, she left a message and then called Desmond to thank him again, too.

She was eating a sandwich at her desk when her phone rang. She thought perhaps Elena was calling her back, but it was Ed to tell her about Larry's uncle.

Excited, she asked Ed to put Larry on the phone. She thanked him and said she'd call Max Green by the end of the day to arrange a visit.

After finishing lunch, she headed to the library. She'd learned who was responsible for setting the fire on the lake and killing the rumrunners, but as far as she was concerned, that was just the beginning.

Next, she was hoping to discover that Etan Canersky had been apprehended and incarcerated, and if, after that, she decided to continue her research, she'd discover more information about Tony, the elusive speakeasy owner.

Within several minutes, she located a brief article with an update about Canersky, but she was disappointed that the search for the elusive criminal continued.

Silver Bay Times

September 15, 1925

An article published by this paper last month that included a description and photo of fugitive Etan Canersky, has resulted in several anonymous tips from residents who believe they may have seen the villain in and around the village of Lighthouse Cove and near Chimney Bluffs.

As a reminder, Canersky set fire to his boat, *Black Duck*, on July 11 which resulted in the drowning deaths of five rumrunners, including two local men, Liam and Harry O'Conner. He is also wanted in Canada for separate crimes.

Despite an extensive manhunt, the rumrunner continues to evade capture. Federal, state and local law enforcement agencies are intensifying their efforts to discover the whereabouts of this diabolical villain in order to apprehend him and find justice for the families of his victims.

Canersky is 5'6" tall, 145 pounds, with short slick-backed blond hair, pale blue eyes, and a small scar above his lip. If you see him, please notify the local police department immediately, but do not approach. He may be armed and is considered extremely dangerous.

CHAPTER 55

Annie had anticipated that the final meeting of the gala committee would last about an hour, but by 10:30 the next morning it was still going strong, the volunteers now arguing about where to place the registration table at the event. Her appointment with Max Green was for 11:00, and the drive would take nearly half an hour.

She smiled brightly. "You have all done such a wonderful job, and I expect the minute you enter the ballroom at the club, the answer will be right in front of you. As much as I'd love to stay, I have an appointment at 11:00. Please carry on and stop by the gift shop on your way out. Martha has gift bags for you with tokens of our appreciation for everything you've done."

She ran into her office, grabbed her purse and headed for her car. She turned on the ignition, took a deep breath, rolled her eyes and thought *"I'm sure everything will work out just fine, but I will be sooo glad when this is over."*

She arrived at the continuing care facility with only a few minutes to spare. A pleasant receptionist escorted her to an airy screened-in porch made bright by terra cotta pots filled with masses of greenery and a variety of summer flowers. A large white ceiling fan rotated slowly, its paddles creating gentle currents of air.

Small, white-haired and with a rosy complexion, Max Green was sitting at a round yellow metal table with a pitcher of iced tea and a plate of cookies. He was wearing khaki shorts, a teal blue golf shirt and white socks and sneakers. She sat, and he reached across the table to place her hands in his, his pale blue eyes shining. Ed said he was a widower, but his large family lived nearby and doted on him.

"Forgive me for not rising, my dear. It takes me a little while to stand and then sit back down." A cane rested beside his chair, and along one wall she noticed a walker.

"Thank you so much for meeting with me, Mr. Green," Annie responded.

"Call me Max, and if you are comfortable, I'll call you Annie. My nephew speaks highly of you and your husband. Now, what can I do for you?"

She spoke of the fire on the lake that killed five rumrunners during Prohibition, the discovery of Tony's Place in the basement at the restaurant, and that despite her efforts to learn more about the proprietor, she'd come to a dead end.

"I was only six when Prohibition ended. I don't remember much about that time. But I was always curious, and as I got older asked my parents a lot of questions. I'll tell you what I know," he said, handing her a glass of tea.

His parents had owned a neighborhood bar and restaurant, a gathering place for the working-class families who lived there. He was the youngest of three children; the other two were girls. His oldest sister was physically and mentally disabled, but at the time no one in the medical community was able to provide a reason for her condition. The income from the business provided a comfortable lifestyle for the family and ongoing medical care for her. Then came Prohibition.

"Unable to serve alcohol, which provided a significant amount of income to us, my father closed the restaurant. He opened a confectionery store that my mother ran, but a speakeasy in the basement of our sprawling cobblestone home provided real income to my family.

"Then a group of mobsters visited and tried pressuring him to sell the speakeasy at a reduced price. When my father refused, they threatened to set fire to the entire building.

"We lived above the confectionery, and desperate to hold onto the business, he asked my mother to bring my sister out to meet them, hoping to play upon their sympathies.

"One of the men was also the father of a disabled child and empathetic, offered a compromise. If my father agreed to purchase all of his liquor from them instead of from his current supplier—naturally, with a markup in cost and a small sum for monthly protection— they'd leave him and our family alone."

"That's horrible."

"He had no choice. It set him back financially, but whatever was left was still better than what they earned at the confectionery or the reduced income that would have resulted from selling the business and leaving us homeless."

"Did they tell you anything about the men? Did they ever mention a man named Tony?"

He shook his head. "Remember, I learned most of this after Prohibition ended. The name isn't familiar, but I think I remember my parents saying that early on there was a head guy; the thugs who came for the payments called him Mr. C."

"Does the name Etan Canersky ring a bell?"

"No. I don't think my parents ever mentioned a last name; they may not have even known it."

He smiled. "This old noggin isn't quite as sharp as it used to be." He rapped his head with his knuckles.

She smiled back. Curious, she asked, "Was your parents' speakeasy ever raided?"

"The speakeasy must have been too small to be on the Feds' radar. It was never raided and after Prohibition ended they reopened the bar and restaurant. It stayed in our family for at least a couple of generations after that."

Annie rose and walked over to the other side of the table, bent down and hugged Max. "Thank you."

"I wish I could have been more helpful."

"Your memory is amazing, Max, and the pieces of the puzzle may be starting to fit together. I think your Mr. C. may have been the man I mentioned, Etan Canersky, who killed the ancestor of a young reporter who was just murdered."

"I read about his death in the paper; how sad for the young man and his family. Please keep me posted."

"I promise to call with updates. Please know how much I appreciate your willingness to speak with me."

On the way back to the office she hummed a 1920s-era song, *Happy Days Are Here Again.*

CHAPTER 56

Annie returned to the museum and was delighted when Martha gave her the 'all-clear'. The volunteers had finished their meeting and driven to the country club to decide where to place the registration table, then prior to decorating the ballroom, ordered lunch at the club's restaurant.

She shook her head. "I truly appreciate all they're doing, but sometimes working with them is a bit exasperating."

Martha replied, "Be patient. By late tomorrow evening this will all be behind you."

Annie walked into her office, read her mail and then checked in with Jason. He said so far the day had been quiet; he expected the usual number of visitors, and the docents taking a group of seniors from Oswego on a tour later that afternoon.

She headed to the library to resume her research; all computers were in use when she arrived. She hadn't eaten lunch so she drove to Marlin's, a small restaurant with outdoor seating and views of the bay, where as she ate, she watched a regatta of sailboats glide by, heading for the channel that went into the lake.

She texted Ed: "*Thanks for suggesting I speak with Max, lovely man. I'll tell you about our conversation tonight. Eating lunch at Marlin's, heading to the library as soon as I'm finished."*

He texted her back and wished her luck. When she returned to the library, one computer had been vacated and she resumed her search. Shortly after, she found another brief newspaper article about the elusive rumrunner. She was disappointed that he still hadn't been captured, but she had a hunch that there was more to the story than the newspaper had indicated.

Silver Bay Times

December 5, 1925

Canersky on the Lam

Etan Canersky, the Canadian rumrunner believed to have killed three Canadian men and two local residents, continues to evade capture despite intensified efforts by federal, state and local law enforcement agencies. The case will remain open.

It has come to the attention of this newspaper that one of the agencies recently received an anonymous tip that Canersky is operating a speakeasy in the county under an assumed name. The authorities have vowed to step up their efforts to locate the villain, optimistic that he soon will be apprehended.

CHAPTER 57

At 5:00 on Saturday night, the DeCleryks arrived at the country club for the museum's fundraising gala. Annie sparkled in a shimmering pale blue, long-waisted beaded chemise, black high-heeled Mary Janes, a crystal cuff bracelet and headband with sequins and a peacock feather. Looking like a contemporary of Al Capone, Ed dressed the part of a 1920s gangster in a black suit and shirt with a red tie, red pocket handkerchief and a gray felt fedora.

The museum's volunteers had transformed the ballroom into a 1920s-era speakeasy with the much-discussed registration table set in the corridor just outside the entrance. Streamers of black, gold and silver crepe paper hung from glittering chandeliers, lights dimmed for mood, with feathery white pampas grass placed in oversized Chinoiserie vases at each corner.

White linen cloths and black napkins adorned the tables, with chairs covered in white satin. Gleaming white dishes sat atop gold chargers, and in the center of each table, silver votive candles flickered in pierced enameled black art deco holders.

Dressed in period costumes, guests lined up at the bar for popular mixed drinks of the era: Sidecars, Old-Fashioneds, Gin Rickeys and Highballs. Servers circulated, carrying platters of pickles and olives, stuffed mushrooms, deviled eggs and a variety of canapés.

Baskets for the silent auction, filled with pottery, books, bottles of wine, gift certificates and theater tickets, were displayed on tables set along one wall in the ballroom; the items for the live auction placed at the back near the auctioneer's podium.

A large screen with slides and videos highlighting the museum's past and present ran continuously throughout the evening.

Outside, flickering like fireflies in motion, multiple strands of fairy lights strung above the patio and woven through potted azalea bushes swayed in the light breeze, illuminated by tall art deco gas lights. In one corner, a four-piece combo played tunes from the jazz age while guests mingled.

At 7:30, 200 guests sat down to a classic 1920s meal of shrimp cocktail, wedge salad with blue cheese dressing, roast beef with horseradish sauce or chicken chasseur, string beans almondine, duchess potatoes, rolls and butter, and for dessert, pineapple upside-down cake with vanilla ice cream.

After dinner, Annie and her board chairperson made a few remarks; she asked Andy Spurling to rise and thanked him for his generous donation of furniture from the speakeasy for the exhibit and silent auction. The silent auction winners were announced, then the live auction bidding began. In short time, at record-high amounts, every item was sold.

The combo on the patio had moved inside during dinner and joined other musicians. Attendees spent the rest of the evening mingling and swing dancing to tunes performed by a Benny Goodman tribute band.

Chris and Elena persuaded his parents, now back from their cruise, to attend the event. They sat at a table with Suzanne, Garrett, his law partner Sheila Caldwell and her spouse, Amy McBride, the pastry chef at Suzanne's parents' restaurant, Callaloo. Desmond and his wife had sent a contribution, indicating that as they aged, large gatherings were less appealing and they'd rather meet Annie and Ed under quieter circumstances.

The DeCleryks wandered over to their table to greet them. For some reason Ed had pictured Greg Kane as an older version of his son, but other than their eyes, they looked nothing alike. Something about him seemed familiar, but he knew they'd never met.

Chris stood, pulled Ed aside and said he and Elena had settled on a date to host the party on the boat; he hoped Ed and Annie would be able to join them; he'd send details.

At the end of the evening after all the guests had gone home, the DeCleryks stayed to help the treasurer tally the proceeds of the silent and live auctions. Annie was ecstatic. The gala had been one of the most successful fundraisers in the museum's history.

CHAPTER 58

After spending Sunday sleeping and relaxing, Annie, now more refreshed, arrived at the museum early on Monday morning to start writing thank-you notes and a report for the next board meeting. She met with the museum's treasurer at 9:00, conducted a staff meeting at 10:00, ate a sandwich at her desk for lunch, and headed to the library to continue her research.

This time, more pieces of the puzzle were revealed. The man Max Green had remembered as Mr. C. was most likely the criminal Etan Canersky; her hunch had been correct. The plot thickened.

Silver Bay Times

March 15, 1926

BREAKING NEWS
Speakeasies Raided, Murderer Escapes

Federal officers from the Bureau of Prohibition successfully raided and closed several speakeasies last night and arrested all but one proprietor, Tony Canetti of Tony's Place, who escaped with the establishment's entire supply of liquor after emptying the safe.

Canetti, aka Etan Canersky, is also the prime suspect in the murder of several rumrunners from Canada and Lighthouse Cove on Lake Ontario in July 1925 and is wanted for an assortment of felonies in Canada.

Despite having cleverly disguised his appearance in order to hide in plain sight, the villain was nevertheless identified by his raspy voice and striking blue eyes by the brother of one of his Canadian victims who recently patronized the speakeasy with a business associate and notified the police.

We have learned that the fugitive was tipped off hours before the raid by a Bureau employee, now in custody, who was on his payroll.

Below is a police artist sketch of the culprit in his current disguise. The man may be armed and is extremely dangerous. If you see him, do not approach and contact the police or FBI immediately.

CHAPTER 59

Annie was thrilled. She called Max who was delighted with the news and reiterated how much he had enjoyed meeting her. Later, over glasses of wine with Ed she said, "I've not only satisfied my curiosity about Tony's Place and who Tony was, but now you can tell Noah's family about what happened to their ancestor. I'll write a summary and make copies of the news articles for you to send to them.

"I am disappointed, though, that I didn't learn what happened to Canersky after he fled the area. I found three more newspaper articles spaced weeks apart; it appears he never got caught and no one knew where he ended up.

"The first said the FBI was following up on some leads and were optimistic Canersky would be apprehended, but the second one indicated they were ending their search and the case had gone cold.

"He seemed to have disappeared into thin air. He may have gone back to Canada, where under his new, assumed name and appearance no one would remember him, or an alternative was that he'd been killed."

"Do you know what happened to his wife and child ?" Ed asked.

184 MURDER AT CHIMNEY BLUFFS

"A little. The third article indicated that the Feds had tracked them down. They relocated to Rochester where she obtained work as a seamstress to support herself and their young son.

"When the police interviewed her, she said she hadn't heard from her husband and knew nothing about his whereabouts. Although she was aware of his work, she'd never been involved with his shady dealings. They believed her.

"I'm so pleased I accomplished what I set out to do, happily much faster than I expected. One thing I can't wrap my head around is why, after he killed those men on the lake, Canersky, even in disguise, stayed in this area rather than escaping to somewhere he was certain not to be caught. He could have just as easily been captured."

Ed responded, "He was certainly cunning. I expect he relished taking risks and deceiving the authorities. He couldn't have chanced going back to Canada on Liam O'Conner's boat; there would have been a BOLO, even then. Plus, he was wanted for several felonies there, too. After he killed the rumrunners, I expect the lake was heavily patrolled by US and Canadian officials hoping to apprehend him."

"I wonder what happened to Liam's boat. If you remember, one of the newspaper articles we read indicated that the authorities were never able to locate it and assumed Canersky had destroyed it."

"I expect that's exactly what happened. He wouldn't have set it on fire; that might have drawn too much attention. My best guess is that when he was confident that he was safe and able to evade capture, he drilled holes in it and it disappeared somewhere in the lake."

"Good point. It's the only explanation that makes sense."

The weather had been perfect that day, clear and sunny with no humidity. Just before dusk, they strolled out to the backyard and sat in the yard to watch the sun, aflame, casting shades of tangerine, grenadine, and molten gold onto the lake as it descended toward the horizon. Later, they watched some shows on PBS, then went upstairs to bed and slept dreamlessly throughout the night.

CHAPTER 60

Over breakfast that next morning, Annie said, "I've been thinking about your investigation, Ed. When you started it, you said there were numerous possibilities about why Noah was killed: the community profile series, his research into what happened to his ancestor, or something more personal.

"You also mentioned the assignment Carol gave him to see what he could dig up on the illegal commercial fishing industry. Maybe that's an avenue you should explore, since you've run into a dead end with everything else."

"I agree, but since we can't access his personal computer and there aren't any notes about it in his work computer, there's not much to go on.

"I'm going to meet with Carrie and Brad later this morning and have decided to work from the police station after that. I'll take Gretchen with me. She's no problem, and I always feel bad about leaving her alone all day.

"After the meeting, I'll check for local charter boat registrations. I expect that most commercial fishing here is conducted in and around Lighthouse Cove because of the preponderance of waterfront restaurants that offer fresh lake fish."

Ed discovered that there were four charter boats that sailed out of Lighthouse Cove. One of the owners was a man named David Canetti.

"Hmmm," he thought. *"Wouldn't it be interesting if he's a descendant of Etan Canersky aka Canetti and, like his infamous ancestor, is also involved in illegal activities."*

He called the four owners; when none answered, most likely because they were out on fishing excursions, he left messages that he wanted to speak with them about Noah's murder, hoping to learn if any of them may have seen something the day he was killed that could help with the investigation.

With the exception of Canetti, by early afternoon he had spoken with the others, but they had nothing to offer, didn't drive black SUVs, and their alibis checked out. He wondered whether Canetti was blowing him off.

He walked into Carrie's office and told her about the phone calls and that Canetti was the only one who hadn't responded.

"You probably can access information about him more easily than I can. Can you do a search for me?"

"I can. I don't have much on my plate today. I'll start right away."

"Thanks. While you're checking, I'm going to take a short break and get Gretchen out for a walk."

"I should have something for you by the time you return."

Carrie walked into the interview room where Ed had been working half an hour later.

"I have information for you. David and Maggie Canetti are a couple in their mid-30s and parents of two young children, a girl and a boy. They met when they were students at SUNY Oswego and live on Cherry Tree Lane just outside Lighthouse Cove.

"She works from home as a graphic artist and he teaches biology at the high school in Williamson, but as you learned, runs a fishing boat charter business in the summer. And he drives a late model black Ford Explorer. Isn't that interesting?"

"It certainly is. If Canetti pads his income as a charter boat captain by supplying local restaurants with lake fish and learned that Noah was asking questions, it's entirely possible that he killed him to protect his lucrative, illegal business. Although it's odd that he'd drive to Rochester to pick Noah up to lure him on the boat."

"It is, but if he did kill Noah, I expect you'll learn the reason for it. As a caution, remember this is a busy season for fisherman. He may not have returned your call because he was out on the lake all day with clients."

"I'll call him again, but this time I'm going to ask him to stop by the station to meet with me. I want to assess his body language when he answers my questions."

CHAPTER 61

David Canetti picked up on the second ring and apologized for not returning Ed's call. As Carrie had thought, he'd been out on his boat with clients. When Ed asked him to stop by the police station before the end of the day, Canetti hesitated, saying he was about to take another charter group out and after that planned on going home. He'd been working since 4:30 that morning and was tired.

He asked if Ed would consider conducting a phone interview, but when Ed responded that the only other option would be to schedule the interview that evening at his home, he agreed to come to the station.

At 4:00, Barb ushered a burly man, about 5'9" tall with short, cropped dark blond hair and hazel eyes, into an interview room. Canetti was wearing jeans, sneakers and a red golf shirt. The two men shook hands and after getting him a Coke from the vending machine, Ed asked him how long he'd been a charter boat captain.

Canetti replied that he'd started the business eight years ago, the summer after his second child was born, in order to make a little extra money to supplement his teaching salary. As he answered the question, he began drumming the fingers of his left hand on the table.

"As I mentioned when we spoke earlier today, I'm investigating the murder of a young news reporter, Noah Pierce. Does that name mean anything to you?"

"Other than hearing about his murder on the news, no."

"What about the name Tony Canetti?"

"Same last name as mine, but it's not familiar. Why?"

"Just curious." Ed explained what Annie had learned during her research and wondered if David's family was related.

Canetti seemed more relaxed and said, "That's cool, but I'm not aware of any members of my family who were rumrunners or owned speakeasies. All my relatives immigrated here after World War II and settled in and around New York City. My grandparents still live on Staten Island in the house they bought when they first married; it's where my dad grew up."

"How did your family end up in this area?" Ed asked.

"My father attended college at the University of Rochester, which is where he met my mother, who's from Jamestown. He works for Paychex, my mom teaches at Monroe Community College, and I grew up in Pittsford."

"When you take your boat out, do you ever sail near Chimney Bluffs?"

The drumming had stopped; by now he had started jiggling a foot. "No, we fish straight north of here. The fishing is fine and it's easier to get back quickly if there's a sudden storm warning."

Ed thought, "*I believe him when he says he isn't related to the rumrunning criminal, but that doesn't mean he isn't fishing commercially and when Noah learned about it, he killed him.*"

"This interview is just routine but still, you seem very nervous. Why is that?"

"I'm not nervous; I'm impatient to get home. It's been a long day."

"You know what, I don't believe you're telling me the truth. What I think is that you're nervous because you're afraid I'm onto you. Are you padding your charter boat income by providing lake fish to local restaurants?"

Canetti's face reddened; he folded his arms across his chest and refused to talk, asking if he needed a lawyer, and continued jiggling his foot. Ed waited patiently without speaking.

He squirmed. "Okay, yes, I've been running a commercial fishing business. I sell to some local restaurants. No big deal. My kids are enrolled in the junior sailing camp for the summer; they both love the water and we come from a boating family. It's a great program but expensive. The extra income helps to pay their tuition. My wife has no idea what I'm doing. She'd be furious with me if she found out."

"You know that it's illegal to fish commercially here, don't you?"

Canetti didn't respond and continued jiggling his foot.

Ed opened the calendar app on his phone and pointed to a date. "This is the day Noah Pierce's body was found on the beach at Chimney Bluffs. One of his newspaper assignments was to investigate illegal commercial fishing on this side of the lake. Did you kill him because he learned about what you are doing?"

"Is that why I'm here? You think I'm a murderer?"

Canetti hung his head, then looked up and said, "I know what I'm doing is illegal, but I didn't kill Noah Pierce. Believe me, I'd never do something like that and have an alibi. My busiest days for the charter business are Wednesday through Sunday, and I fish on Tuesdays for the restaurants. I take every Monday off to volunteer at my kids' camp, helping the younger ones learn to sail. We get a small tuition break."

He opened his phone to his contacts. "Here's the name and phone number of the camp director. He'll be able to verify I was there."

"My sole reason for interviewing you is because of the murder investigation, so at this point, if your alibi checks out, what you're doing isn't pertinent to my case, and I won't report you to the authorities. That said, I advise you to find ways to build up your charter business and stop the illegal fishing.

"It's only a matter of time until the Coast Guard gets wind of it, and you'll get caught. If you do, not only will you lose your charter license but possibly also your teaching job. I don't think either of those consequences would be good for your family."

Canetti nodded. "I know what I've been doing is wrong, and it weighs on me all the time. I'll tell my customers I can't supply them with fish anymore. My family needs me, and as you suggested, I'll work a little harder on building up the charter business."

He sighed. "I guess I needed that kick in the rear. Thank you."

Ed stood up and reached across the table and held out his hand. "Good luck."

Canetti stood and shook it. "Thank you, thank you again."

Taking another big sigh, he left the room.

CHAPTER 62

Threads woven together unraveled. False hopes and disappointments. Yet again, the case had gone cold. Ed, frustrated and needing to put some distance between himself and the investigation, decided, with Annie's encouragement, to register for a seminar on new technology used in forensic investigations that was being sponsored by the Criminal Consultants' Association of America at the Drake Hotel in Chicago.

The deadline had passed, but he knew one of the organizers, and when he explained why he had waited until the last minute, his contact said he could attend but would be charged a small late fee. He checked flights from Rochester to Chicago; fortunately several seats were still available on American Airlines.

He called Annie.

"Hi, Annie, I can attend the seminar. I'll have to pay a late fee, but it's not much, and I think it will do me a lot of good to get out of town for a couple of days. Listen, I have an idea. It starts at 7:30 on Saturday morning and ends at 3:00. Why don't you come with me? You could work Friday morning. There's a 1:00 flight on American Airlines, and we'd arrive at the hotel by mid-afternoon.

"We could have a leisurely dinner at the hotel that night, and while I'm at the seminar the next day you'd have time to yourself. Afterwards, we could spend the rest of the day together."

"I'd love to, but you know how busy the summers are here, and I'm not sure I can take time to be away right now. Jason has been working most Sundays, but he's taking this one off for a family event. I'll need to be at the museum by 1:30 to help volunteers with the concert; the crowds have been quite large this year."

"I don't think that will be a problem. There's a return flight that will get us back by late Sunday morning."

"You know what, I've been wanting to see some exhibits at the Art Institute. I could spend most of the day there, eat lunch at the café, and then do a little shopping on my way back to the hotel. I'll call Sandy. If she can watch Gretchen, I'm in. I'll call you back in a few minutes."

Ed's phone rang. "Sandy will pick Gretchen up on Friday morning. Go ahead and make the arrangements."

Ed had just purchased airline tickets when his phone rang again.

"Hi, Ed."

"Eric, how are you?"

"I'm well, thanks. I wanted to give you an update on Belinda Corey. I called and said I was checking in to see how she was doing after our conversation at the supermarket and invited her to have dinner with us last night.

"She accepted, and after we put the kids to bed, we sat outside on the deck and drank some wine. After a couple glasses and a bit of gentle encouragement, she opened up. She's overwhelmed by the changes in her life: her parents' divorce, the death of her grandmother and her dog, and the end of the relationship with Noah and his untimely death.

"She admitted to stalking him, hoping she could change his mind about the breakup. She confessed she was looking for sympathy and attention when she informed me that she and Noah had been engaged.

"All that loss in such a short time has taken a toll on her. The only thing that seems to be keeping her sane is her job; she loves working at the childcare center."

Eric said he'd suggested she get professional help, and she agreed. He talked with his friend at the psych department that morning who recommended a therapist; she'd scheduled an appointment for the following week. The therapist worked with a psychiatrist who would prescribe short-term medication if necessary.

"That's great news. What you and Lily did was very kind. I feel sorry for her and am happy she'll be getting the help she needs."

"Thank you, Ed, for caring enough to mention her situation to me."

The two men ended the call, then Ed started thinking about what he would pack for the trip.

CHAPTER 63

The flight left on time; the DeCleryks arrived at the hotel by mid-afternoon. After unpacking, taking a short walk and changing into dressy attire, they took the elevator to Coq d'Or, a landmark restaurant that had opened at the hotel in December 1933 after the end of Prohibition. A pianist sat at a grand piano, playing classic tunes from the 1930s and '40s.

The couple spent the evening enjoying their meals, happy to be able to be together without the pressures of the investigation for Ed and the hectic pace of summer activities for Annie.

Then, hand-in-hand, they took the elevator to their room. Annie surprised Ed by changing into a filmy peignoir. He smiled and pulled his wife onto the bed, where for several minutes before falling into a deep sleep, they reminded each other of their love and why their relationship had endured for decades.

The next morning, they ordered room service for breakfast, and after showering and dressing, Ed headed to the conference.

Before starting out to the Art Institute, Annie went to the lobby and stood in line waiting to speak with the concierge, hoping he'd be able to offer suggestions for activities she and Ed might enjoy after the conference ended. The line was moving slowly, so she decided she'd check back with him after lunch.

The concierge was sitting alone at his desk when she returned. She approached him and asked for suggestions about what she and Ed could do for the rest of the afternoon. When he learned she ran a museum and historical society and about her interest in Prohibition, he said, "If you're up for walking, you might enjoy our speakeasy tour."

"I've probably already walked about five miles so far today, but I'm not tired and I think my husband might enjoy the exercise. He's been sedentary for most of the day."

He handed her a brochure. "The tour starts at 3:30 two miles from here and takes about three hours. You'll visit four speakeasies and at the end have an option for dinner at the Exchequer Restaurant and Pub, where Al Capone and his cronies dined. If you're interested, I can make the dinner reservation for you, too."

"Oh, my goodness, that would be perfect."

She texted Ed. By now, the conference had ended; he was in their room. She texted back: "*I'll be right up.*"

She explained, "The concierge called ahead and let the tour guide know we're coming, but we'll have to hurry, it starts soon. I'm sorry, I should have asked you before I made the arrangements if you're too tired to take a three-hour tour. The brochure indicated it's a mile long."

"I've been sitting all day; I'd like to stretch my legs. The tour sounds perfect. You might get information about speakeasies and Prohibition that you could include in your exhibit."

Annie called the concierge to thank him. He said two tickets would be waiting for them at the tour site and he'd make the dinner reservation. They didn't have much time to spare, instead of walking he suggested they take a cab. By the time they arrived in the lobby, the cab driver was standing at the door of the lobby waiting for them.

CHAPTER 64

Their guide, a woman in her 30s named Ashley Jackson, had bachelor's and master's degrees in American studies from Northwestern University, with a focus on the 1920s and 30s.

She explained the history of speakeasies in Chicago and gave colorful stories of the city's seedy Prohibition past and the lengths the gangsters took to get their hands on illegal booze.

They visited Capone's, Torrio's, Nitti's, and the last on the tour, a place called Canery's. At each stop, a bar had been set up where they could purchase light snacks and iconic mixed drinks, and the guide provided them with information about the gangster who owned the speakeasy.

When they entered Canery's, the docent gave the group a few minutes to look around then gathering them together asked, "Before we started this tour, how many of you recognized the name Al Capone?"

All raised their hands.

"What about Frank Nitti?" Again, they all raised their hands.

"John Torrio?" About half raised their hands.

"Tony Canery?" None raised their hands.

She continued. "Not surprising. Canery was not well known because unlike the others, he wasn't as notorious, at least not here. But his past in many ways was even more fascinating than theirs.

"Tony started his career as a rumrunner in Canada, transporting liquor across Lake Ontario to Chimney Bluffs, now a state park, and other hideaways near Lighthouse Cove, a village located between Rochester and Syracuse in New York."

Annie glanced at Ed and then raised her hand.

"Yes?"

"Excuse me for interrupting. Was Tony Canery his given name?"

"No. I was getting to that. He was born with the name Etan Canersky."

She grabbed Ed's hand.

Ashley pulled a black and white photo from her file and showed it to the group.

"Even though this photo is not in color, you can see that Canersky had slicked-back light hair and very pale eyes. He was clean shaven with a scar above his upper lip.

"One night in July 1925, he sailed across the lake with his men to meet up with rumrunners from the US. Strong evidence suggests he held all the men hostage on his boat, set it on fire, and while they were jumping into the water to avoid being burned to death but subsequently drowned, he escaped on the Americans' boat with the money and the liquor. Then he disappeared."

She paused. "Canersky, who knew how to get out of a bad situation, was also a master of disguise."

She pulled out a drawing showing a man with dark, straight, slicked back, and a dark pencil mustache. "Other than perhaps the eyes, does this man resemble Canersky?"

The group shook their heads.

She smiled. "This is a man named Tony Canetti, who Canersky became when he settled, hiding in plain sight, near Lighthouse Cove. Amazing, isn't it?"

"There, with the money and liquor he stole, he opened a speakeasy and with approval from the Rochester mob, employed a cadre of enforcers to shakedown owners of smaller establishments who were forced to purchase their liquor from them or suffer the consequences."

She continued. "As time went on, a brother of one of the Canadian victims of the fire visited the speakeasy and, despite the disguise, recognized the man and tipped off the Feds, who raided his and other speakeasies one night soon after.

"Unfortunately, he evaded capture; a mole within the Bureau tipped him off. Yet again he fled, this time to Chicago, taking all the money in the safe and all the liquor, and abandoning his wife and their young son.

"The Rochester mob arranged for him to meet Al Capone. He changed his name, this time to Tony Canery. You can see the pattern here. While he kept the mustache, he let his hair grow, and dyed it reddish brown. Colored contacts had recently been invented, he also changed his eye color and started wearing glasses. Because he was small and wiry, he added lifts to his shoes to make himself look taller and employed a tailor who was connected to the mob to add extra padding to his suits.

"A narcissistic psychopath, Capone rewarded those who were deferential to him. Canery knew how to play him. As a measure of his respect, he offered the mobster the money and liquor he'd taken from his speakeasy.

"Capone refused, but impressed with his respectful attitude, hired him as an enforcer. The two men developed a close bond and after several months, the mobster gave Canery permission to open his own speakeasy, the one you are standing in now."

Annie raised her hand. "I run the historical society and museum in Lighthouse Cove. I've been doing research for an upcoming exhibit on Prohibition and have spent weeks poring through old newspaper articles to piece together most of what you've been telling us, but the information I got is not nearly as complete. How did you find all of this?"

"The company I work for, which conducts other historical tours, has a team of researchers. We want the information to be as accurate as possible."

The woman handed Annie her card and said, "Call me if I can help you with your exhibit."

She thanked her. "Did his family ever join him?"

"No, they never saw him again. He had a mistress here, a showgirl; they were together for many years."

A tall man with bright red hair and a bushy beard raised his hand. "What happened to Canery? Was he ever apprehended?"

"No, not that we're aware of. After Prohibition ended, he closed the speakeasy but continued to work as an enforcer for the Chicago mob. Several years later he changed his identity and appearance again, left his mistress and fled to California, but after that the trail went cold. There's no information about when or how he died."

The concierge at the hotel had made a reservation for Annie and Ed at the Exchequer for 6:45. After the tour ended, they walked the two blocks to the restaurant.

Annie sighed. "He was brilliant, Ed. Canersky hid in plain sight all those years, changing his appearance and name, but always keeping the first four letters of the surname he was born with. He was playing a joke on law enforcement, and by changing his looks he was always one step ahead of them. What a diabolical and fascinating man. In a strange way I admire him.

"I'm so glad you convinced me to join you. This has been an amazing day. I wish your seminar had been weeks ago; it would have saved me countless hours at the library."

The couple didn't speak again until they were seated at the restaurant. Annie asked Ed about his day. He replied that while he had learned a lot, forensic techs were the ones who would typically use the technology, although he had a better understanding of the process.

They chatted amiably while they ate and later hailed a cab to the hotel. The next morning, after a deep sleep and a good breakfast, they caught an early flight back to Rochester.

CHAPTER 65

Ed was frustrated. He hadn't been able to apprehend Noah Pierce's killer; every person of interest had an alibi and there were no additional suspects.

That night, sitting in bed reading, Ed said to Annie, "I don't know why, but there's still something about this case that seems familiar."

"Ed, remember how we used to watch those cold case shows on TV? Maybe one of those reminded you of this investigation."

He had an 'Aha!' moment, leaned across the bed and kissed Annie.

"There are many reasons why I married you. You just helped me figure it out. It wasn't a cold case on TV; it was a cold case here. Do you remember Tom Ellison, the chief of police who preceded me?"

"Of course I do. He and his wife moved to Florida a year or so after he retired, but before then I seem to recall that you and he spent a lot of time together."

"That's right. Tom took me under his wing; we met once a month for lunch at Louise's. At one of those lunches, he said his biggest regret was not being able to solve a cold case, a young female journalist with the *Silver Bay Times* whose body had been found on the beach at Chimney Bluffs about 25 years ago.

"She was assaulted, not sexually, and the cause of death was by drowning. Like Noah, she'd been injured before she hit the water. She wasn't working on any assignments that would have put her in harm's way. Tom believed her murder was personal, but he never figured out who killed her."

"Are you thinking Noah's killer could be the same person? That murder was a long time ago."

'It's possible, depending on the killer's age at the time."

"Why don't you call Carol Smalley. She may have been working at the newspaper when it happened and remembers something about it."

"Great idea. I'll call her in the morning."

The editor said she'd been working as a reporter for a newspaper in Warren, Pennsylvania when that murder occurred. He called Carrie and asked if she could assign someone to search the cold case files at the police station.

For some unexplained reason Carrie was testy. "I think you are looking for a needle in the haystack, Ed. I can't drop everything, and as you know, we don't exactly have a large staff. I'll get to it when I can."

He sighed, reminding himself to be patient. "I don't expect you to drop everything, Carrie, but I'm running out of options. If something doesn't turn up soon, Noah's death will be filed away as a cold case just like the other."

CHAPTER 66

Suzanne and Garrett lived in a cottage that backed up to an inlet from the bay. Early on Saturday evening, Chris and Elena Kane anchored their boat at the dock behind it to collect their friends for the dinner cruise.

The DeCleryks carried a waterproof tote they normally kept on their pontoon that contained packets of facial tissue, a roll of paper towels, some plastic bags and a Swiss Army knife for emergencies. They'd added two bottles of wine and sweaters, should the evening get cool. Suzanne and Garrett had also brought a tote, almost identical to the DeCleryk's, with light jackets and homemade coconut cake for dessert.

Chris said, "Suzanne, there's a refrigerator in the cabin; you can store the dessert there, and Ed, I'll take the wine to the upper deck where we'll be having drinks and dinner."

"What should we do with our totes?" Ed asked.

"Put them in the cabin; it'll give us more room upstairs. You can always come back down here if you need anything later this evening."

A clear sky and light wind made for perfect sailing. After an hour of sampling a charcuterie platter and drinking wine, they anchored near Crescent Beach, and Chris grilled a simple meal of chicken, corn and a medley of summer squashes. They sat at a table while they ate, enjoying the delicious food, balmy night and good conversation. Suddenly, the wind picked up and the temperature dropped.

Ed noticed Annie shivering and asked if she wanted him to get her sweater. She nodded, and saying he'd be back shortly, he walked downstairs, tripping over the threshold as he entered the cabin.

One of his shoelaces had become untied. He bent down to tie it and noticed what appeared to be a travel coffee mug under one of the benches.

"Well, well, well," he thought. *"What do we have here?"*

He stood, grabbed a paper towel from his tote and carefully pulled out the mug. The design on front was a white Yin on a black background. He remembered Brad saying that he and the other investigators found a mug with the Yang symbol in Noah's kitchen. He believed it to be one of a set—the one with the Yin missing.

Pulling two plastic bags from the tote, he placed the mug into one, and with his Swiss Army knife, scraped some carpet threads into the other and hid both in the bottom. He decided to use the head, and when he came out, Chris was standing in the doorway.

CHAPTER 67

"Everything okay, Ed? Annie was starting to get worried about what was taking you so long. I came down to get the dessert."

He grinned. "Yep. I tripped on the threshold and one of my shoelaces became untied. After I tied it, I decided to use the head. Suzanne and Garrett's tote is almost identical to ours; they're both from the museum gift shop, so I had to look inside each to find Annie's sweater. I'll take ours upstairs to avoid confusion when we leave. I apologize if I worried everyone."

Chris looked at him strangely but didn't say anything. He got the cake out of the refrigerator; then the two men climbed up to the top deck, where Suzanne cut and served the cake.

Wanting to divert the conversation, Ed said, "Nice boat. A trawler?"

"Yes, it's great for cruising and partying and it's big enough for a couple of people to fish. We love it, but we've been having some problems with the radio, which is concerning.

"We replaced it earlier this summer, but when I checked to make sure everything was in working order before we set off this afternoon, I noticed it was broken again.

"I'll have to call the repair shop and see if there's a permanent solution. Fortunately, we always keep our cell phones with us when we sail, and unless we're far out on the lake, there's usually some reception. That's why we decided to stay on the bay tonight.

"A life preserver is also missing. There should be eight, but because there are six of us tonight, we're fine. An attendant at the marina cleans the boat after it's used. It may have been tossed by accident."

"Where do you keep the boat?" Annie asked.

Elena replied, "We rent space at a marina on Irondequoit Bay. It's a short drive from our house. Are you boaters?"

"We are. We keep a pontoon at a marina in Lighthouse Cove. But Ed's a much more experienced boater than I am. I've never been comfortable taking it out alone like he sometimes does. I'm not confident I'd be able to handle it in an emergency."

"I feel the same way," Elena responded. "Chris, on the other hand, is such a good sailor that when he wants to mull over an upcoming trial or just to get away for a few hours, he'll take it out by himself, too. I envy that; it must be very meditative."

On their way to Lighthouse Cove after dinner, Chris mentioned that their children were having a sleepover at his grandparents' house; they were going to spend the night at their cottage on White Pelican Island.

They kept a car there; a causeway connected the island to the mainland. They'd leave the boat in the boathouse and drive the car to Webster early the next morning to attend their 11-year-old daughter's soccer game. After the game, with kids in tow, they'd drive the car back to the island, spend the night and sail the boat back to Irondequoit the next day.

When they pulled into Suzanne and Garrett's dock, Suzanne asked the two couples if they'd like to come in for a nightcap.

"We'd better get going," Chris said. "We prefer not sailing when it's too dark."

"We'll take a raincheck," Annie said, concerned about Ed, who had been quiet and looked a little peaked. "I think my husband might be ready to go home, too."

Their guests thanked the Kanes and stood and waved as they sailed away.

Annie said, "You seem a little off, Ed. Are you feeling okay?"

"Just tired. It's been a busy week, and I can't seem to get my mind off the investigation."

Garrett asked, "How it's going?"

"It's been frustrating, but based on some recent evidence, I think we may be getting closer to solving the crime."

CHAPTER 68

Back in the car, Annie said, "Ed, what was that all about? What are you not telling me?"

"I'll explain over a cup of tea when we get home."

After letting Gretchen out, Ed brewed mint tea, poured it into two cups, and the couple sat in the yard on chairs facing the water. The wind had calmed down, but it was still cool. Annie pulled her sweater tightly around her body.

"Okay, husband of mine. Spill the beans."

He walked back inside and returned with the tote. He opened it and pulled out the bags that contained the mug and carpet threads.

"I found this mug under a bench in the cabin on the Kane's boat. It matches the description of the one Brad thinks went missing from Noah's kitchen. Mike said he found marine carpet threads embedded in the soles of his shoes, I scraped some threads from the cabin floor.

"I'll send both to the crime lab on Monday for verification, but I'm almost certain Noah was on that boat when he died. But with whom and why?"

Annie responded, "It couldn't have been Elena. I believed her when she said she never takes the boat out. Chris' parents were on a cruise, and his grandfather is in his late 80s and apparently not quite as fit as he used to be, so unless the Kanes loaned it to someone, the only explanation is that Noah was on that boat with Chris."

"That makes the most sense, but I don't believe Chris killed him. There was only one phone call between them and that was weeks ago; no texts, emails or notes in Noah's files that he'd even begun to develop questions or get background information for the interview. Chris also has an alibi. He was at a staff meeting at a diner at 7:30 the morning Noah was killed. I verified it. He couldn't be two places at once, and Mike's relatively certain about the time of death."

"Ed, do you remember me telling you that when I took Elena to lunch at the Bistro how strangely Terri reacted when she realized Elena and Chris were married? And that when Elena asked her if she knew Chris, she said she might have met him when she was a server at a restaurant near the courthouse in Rochester?"

"I do."

"I didn't say anything to you about it that night, but I'm positive Terri was lying, and while Elena pretended to accept her explanation, I'm pretty sure she thought so, too. I could tell how uncomfortable she was."

"I can see where this is going."

"Yes, I'm sure you do. Quite frankly, I wondered if, as she said, Terri met him at the restaurant, but there was more to it than that—they had an affair. She's beautiful and was young and impressionable and might have easily succumbed to an older, powerful, handsome man's advances. He seems to adore Elena, but we don't know what their relationship was like years ago.

"Noah and Terri aren't that far apart in age. Perhaps they know some of the same people, and Noah ran into someone who, when he mentioned his assignment to interview community leaders for the paper and that one of those was Chris, responded that the DA isn't the poster child everyone thinks he is; a friend of his had an affair with him and it ended badly."

"If that happened, you think Noah said something to Chris about it?"

"I can't imagine he'd gossip. Maybe he doubted the information was true and wanted to alert Chris that he'd heard something about him that could affect his family and career. Perhaps he visited Chris in his office, indicating he wanted to speak with him privately about a personal matter."

"Annie, how could that be a motive for murder?"

"Hear me out, Ed. Remember, at dinner Elena said he sometimes takes the boat out to be alone when he's mulling over an upcoming trial. He suggests they discuss the matter on the boat—they'd have plenty of privacy—and to cover his tracks, he tells Elena he's struggling with a work issue and is going to go for a pre-dawn boat ride to clear his head. He takes a change of clothes with him and says he'll be at the diner with his staff at 7:30, which you verified.

"He picks Noah up just before dawn and drives him to the marina where they board the boat and sail into the bay or maybe even the lake. Then something goes sideways. Maybe Chris says he doesn't trust Noah to keep the information to himself. Noah's offended; there's an altercation. Even if what happened was an accident, Chris knows if he reports it there will be a scandal and lots of questions asked.

"At some point, Noah may have mentioned the research he was doing to find out about what happened to his ancestor, and Chris realizes it's a perfect opportunity to get rid of him and have investigators think his death was related to that project.

"He calls someone who owes him a favor, perhaps someone from his past he decided not to prosecute. That person meets him at the marina and transports Noah, who is injured and in no shape to fight back, to Chimney Bluffs where he tosses him into the water and then returns the boat to the marina. While that's happening, Chris is meeting with his staff at the diner. The perfect alibi."

"Sounds like a crime show on TV, Annie. And while it's certainly plausible, I still don't believe Chris is our killer."

"Even if you're right, you have an obligation to question him, if only to rule him out. But then if he didn't do it, who did?"

"No clue. I'll call Carrie on Monday morning with an update and take the mug and carpet threads to the crime lab for analysis. If they verify the mug was Noah's, and threads match the ones in his shoes, I'll schedule an interview with him. Something is very odd about this entire situation, and I will get to the bottom of it."

CHAPTER 69

Ed waited for the results at the crime lab on Monday morning. An hour later, the technicians verified that the prints on the mug were Noah's, and the fibers matched the ones found on his shoes. He texted Carrie, and she asked him to stop by the police station as soon as he returned to Lighthouse Cove to meet with her and Brad.

He hadn't eaten that morning, and he knew the police chief always appreciated coffee from Bistro Louise. He parked his car in front of the café and ordered to-go cups of black for himself and Brad, mocha latte for the police chief, and a half dozen freshly baked chocolate chip muffins. Terri wasn't in yet; Louise, looking frazzled, took his order.

"You look exhausted, Louise; are you okay?"

"I am exhausted, Ed. Doing all the baking and running the café are taking a toll on me. I'm not so young anymore and don't have the energy I used to. I've purchased the small building next door and would like to find a partner; someone who can run the bakery side of the business for me. If you can think of anyone who might be interested, ask that they contact me."

Ed thought about Amy McBride, but she already had a job she loved, and he couldn't imagine her wanting to leave it or commute from Rochester to Lighthouse Cove. "I will, and I hope your day gets better."

A few minutes later, handing the beverages to the two other investigators, he set the bag of muffins on the table. Carrie beamed.

"You're a lifesaver, Ed. Natasha was up all night with an earache; Matt and I are both exhausted. Coffee always helps, so does sugar. My dad is taking her to the doctor while my mom looks after Arturo. And by the way, I apologize for my testiness the other day when you asked me to search for the cold case files. We'd been up the night before, Arturo this time, with a poison ivy rash."

"Understand, and no offense taken. Annie and I have been there; it's tough raising kids in a two-career family."

Brad reported that he and Mia had caught the vandals who set the fires and graffitied the bathhouse and snack bar at the beach —teenagers from Fair Haven who, after ingesting a large amount of marijuana and beer, decided to have a little fun. One of the kids was in the system; when they tracked hm down he outed the others.

They agreed it was time to schedule an interview with Chris Kane. They didn't want to tip him off that he was a suspect. Instead, Ed called and asked if he and Brad could get his advice about something to do with the case, dissembling by saying that the Wayne County DA was away on vacation.

"Happy to help, Ed. I have a busy schedule today, but I can squeeze you in at 11:30. Will that be enough time? We can do an early lunch; I'll order sandwiches."

"That works. Thanks. See you soon."

Ed left the office, drove home to let Gretchen out and called Annie. Brad picked him up at 10:30 and they headed to the city. They agreed that Ed would take the lead in questioning.

CHAPTER 70

They parked in the lot across the street from the courthouse. After going through a metal detector and surrendering their cell phones and Brad's gun, they were escorted to the district attorney's office.

Chris greeted them and gestured to a table where a plate of sandwiches and drinks had been placed. "Help yourselves. I know you want some advice about the case; how can I help you?"

Ed responded, "I'll get straight to the point, Chris. I found Noah's travel mug in the cabin on your boat on Saturday night. Can you tell me why it was there?"

"Are you sure it's his?"

"I am. The crime lab verified his prints on the mug, and I scraped threads from the carpet on your boat that match the ones the ME found embedded in his shoes. So, what was he doing on your boat?"

"I have no idea. I think I told you we'd never met. And what gave you the right to snoop in my cabin without a search warrant?"

"I wasn't snooping; I found it when I bent down to tie my shoe. It was pretty much in plain sight and there was suspicion of a crime. I had every right to take it."

"Ed, I truly don't understand why you would even consider me a suspect."

"I'll get to that. Do you happen to know a woman named Terri McGovern?"

Chris was quiet for several seconds. "Yes, I do. But I haven't seen her in years. What does she have to do with the murder?

"Wait, don't answer that. I think I know what this is about, and you couldn't be more off base. You think she and I had an affair and our young reporter found out about it. He contacted me, I lured him onto my boat because I didn't trust him to keep the brewing scandal to himself and killed him to save my reputation. Sounds like a plot for one of those cozy mysteries, doesn't it?"

"Not bad. You're on the right track."

He laughed bitterly. "If it weren't so offensive, it would be funny. Now, let's get back to the question of how I know Terri. First, to get it out of the way, if you knew me better, you'd know I adore my wife and would never be unfaithful to her."

"Then why did you hesitate to answer my question?"

He sighed. "Because she's not even remotely involved with any of this. I was the assistant DA assigned to her case when she was arrested for shoplifting."

Ed and Brad glanced at each other.

Chris explained. She had stolen about $300 worth of costume jewelry from a boutique when she was living in Rochester. The shop owner identified her because she'd purchased items with a credit card there at another time.

"When I met with her and the public defender, she was terrified, promised she'd never steal again, and pleaded with me not to send her to jail. As a first offender, that wouldn't have happened, but she was looking at probation, community service and restitution. I believed her; her remorse was genuine, and I thought that this was most likely a one-time transgression. I was willing to drop the charges if the shop owner agreed.

"He did, but only if she paid him back. She didn't have the money; instead of selling the items, she'd given them to her friends who thought she'd bought them gifts and had no idea they were stolen.

"She was working as a server at Soleil, an upscale restaurant near the courthouse; her wages would have been garnished. We were pretty sure she'd be fired before that happened; no restaurant would employ a thief."

"My sense was she was basically a good kid who had done something stupid. I wanted her to have a second chance. I went home and talked with Elena and we agreed to take care of paying the shop owner anonymously. Now that I reflect back on it, I probably could have lost my job, but we wanted to help.

"Elena sent a cashier's check for the full amount. I never mentioned it to Terri's attorney who seemed surprised that the charges had been dropped and speculated that perhaps the shop owner had a change of heart. I didn't disabuse him of that, and we scheduled a meeting with Terri.

"She was relieved and very thankful for the reprieve. I suggested that she find a constructive way to spend her time so she wouldn't get into any more trouble, maybe do some volunteering. I was pleasantly surprised when she agreed and asked for suggestions.

"When I asked about her interests, she said that she had taken pottery making classes in high school and had really enjoyed the experience. I said that my wife and I had a friend who ran a community center in the city and was looking for volunteers to help start up an art program. She committed to spending several hours a week there when she wasn't waitressing, teaching classes to pre-teens.

"Our friend reported that it was a perfect fit, the kids loved her, and she continued volunteering until she moved back to Lighthouse Cove. I understand she's an accomplished potter now, and to my knowledge she never got in trouble again.

"You may be wondering why I was so quick to catch on that you believed she and I had been romantically involved. It's because of what transpired the evening Elena got home after spending the afternoon with Annie. She was very quiet and somewhat distant; when I kissed her she pulled away.

"There's a lot of trust between us, and her reaction totally surprised me. When I asked what was wrong, at first she wouldn't talk about it. Then she said when she and Annie had lunch that day at a café in Lighthouse Cove, Annie introduced her to the server, a woman named Terri McGovern.

"When Terri put two-and-two together and realized that Elena and I were married, she reacted strangely. Elena asked if she knew me; she responded that I'd been a regular customer at the restaurant where she worked. I'm disturbed and angry that Terri didn't tell my wife the truth, that I'd helped her out of a jam at one point when she was younger. If she had, what transpired that evening wouldn't have occurred."

"Maybe she was embarrassed and ashamed and didn't want Annie to know about it."

"That makes sense, but it caused emotional distress for my wife, and that's unforgivable."

"Anyway, Elena was confused by her response. I had been to Soleil for lunch with some colleagues, just once, shortly after I started working at the courthouse and before Terri became a server there. I told my wife I thought the restaurant was pretentious, overly expensive, and that I had no desire to go back, and I didn't. Naturally, she wondered if I'd lied to her or if I hadn't, why Terri had.

"She asked straight out if we'd had an affair. In her heart she knows I'd never cheat on her, but I certainly can understand why she might think that. That's when I disclosed that Terri was the young woman whom we'd helped after she was arrested for shoplifting.

"I remember telling Terri that other than her attorney and me, no one else knew about what happened, and that because of her age and that we believed her when she said she'd never do anything like that again, even the shop owner promised not to discuss the case with anyone. She could move forward with her life without fear of reprisal.

"When Elena and I decided to pay the shop owner back, I never mentioned any of the specifics of the case to her, just that a young woman had gotten into trouble and I wanted to help."

"Noah entered someone's SUV around 5:00 the morning he died. Where were you at that time?" Ed asked.

"I was at urgent care from 4:00 to 5:30 with our seven-year-old, Amelia. She had spiked a fever earlier that evening, was sick to her stomach in the middle of the night and complained about a very sore throat. We decided not to wait until morning to get treatment for her, and I'm glad we did. It turns out she had a strep infection. I can give you the name of the doctor we saw."

"We decided it would make more sense for me to take Amelia than for Elena to do it. I figured the urgent care center wouldn't be all that busy that early in the morning, and I'd be able to get to work in time for my 7:30 meeting. Elena had already committed to driving our kids and our neighbors' kids to summer camp that morning where our oldest works as a junior counselor."

Convinced that Chris didn't kill Noah, Ed now suspected he knew who did, although he had no idea why.

"Just out of curiosity, does anyone in your family drive an SUV?"

"I do. A light gray Honda Pilot."

"Elena?"

"She drives a white Ford minivan—remember, we have four children."

"What about your parents and grandparents?"

"My grandfather. A black Acura MDX. Why?"

CHAPTER 71

"Because the cameras in front of Noah's apartment filmed him getting into a late model, black SUV the morning he was killed. I believe you when you say you didn't kill him; I never was completely convinced of your guilt to begin with. But I'm almost certain your grandfather was responsible for his death."

"Seriously? Did you identify the vehicle as an Acura MDX? What about the license plates? This is preposterous. To my knowledge Noah and my grandfather never met and had only spoken two times."

"That's what your grandfather told me, too, and I believed him at the time. The cameras outside Noah's building didn't show the make or model of the car or the plates in the front or back of the car, but it definitely was a black, late model SUV. If your grandfather didn't do it, why did we find evidence of the crime on your boat?"

"Is there someone else who has access to it? We're pretty sure it wasn't Elena; she said she never takes it out by herself, and she's way too tiny to have injured Noah and then tossed him into the water. Besides, what would her motive be?"

The DA was quiet for several seconds, then responded, "As much as I hate to admit it, you could be right. But Noah's death had to be an accident. My grandfather is not a large man and he's in his 80s. He wouldn't have the strength to do what you're accusing him of, and I'm certain he would never intentionally kill anyone."

"Did you have any contact with him the day of the murder?"

Chris sighed. "I did. My grandmother was away visiting my sister and her family. As you know, my parents were away on a cruise. I think I told you when we had drinks at Rumrunners that I called my grandfather every morning before he left for work, just to make sure he was okay.

"When I was back in my office after the staff meeting, about 8:45, I called him on his cell phone, and when he didn't answer, his landline. When he didn't pick up, I left a message."

"Were you concerned?"

"Not at the time. He can be a bit absent-minded, and I thought maybe he'd turned off his phone before he went to bed and for some reason didn't hear the landline ring. He called back an hour later, apologized and said he'd left the cell phone in his car the night before and he'd forgotten to place the landline back in its cradle, and the battery had died.

"He said he was calling from work, but it sounded like he was driving. I heard the blast of a boat horn in the background. When I asked him about it, he said I probably was hearing trucks entering the parking bays from overnight runs, the drivers were honking their horns to each other in greeting. He could hear them, too; his windows were open. But I know the difference between a boat blast and a truck horn."

"You wondered if he lied, didn't you?"

"I must admit, a little. But when I couldn't figure out why, I let it go."

"How skilled a boater is he? Could he have made it back from Chimney Bluffs in less than two hours and was leaving the marina when he called you back?"

"I suppose so. Boating used to be one of his hobbies. While Elena and I primarily use the trawler, it's jointly owned by my family along with a cabin cruiser, pontoon and a small motorboat. My grandparents prefer the cruiser, but he was adept at sailing all the boats.

"A year or so ago he started having some problems navigating and was careless about safety issues. After one slightly unnerving experience, he promised us he and my grandmother wouldn't take any of the boats out unless one of us was with them. It's making me sick to think that he had anything to do with Noah's death; he shouldn't have been on that boat in the first place."

"Are there secrets about your grandfather Noah may have learned while he was doing research about your family?"

He shook his head. "None that I can think of."

Then he paused. "Although now that you mention it, I remember a conversation with my grandmother years ago, when before he retired my grandfather flew out to San Diego with my father on a business trip.

"My mother decided to join them at the last minute. A former college roommate lived there, and while they'd kept in touch, they hadn't seen each other for many years.

"One evening while they were away, we hired a sitter for the kids and took my grandmother out to dinner. At one point, we discussed how blessed we'd all been with happy marriages. I asked her what the key to her and Grandpa's success was. They'd been married more than fifty years.

"She said they never kept secrets from each other, that trusting and respecting your mate is important, and she respected Grandpa more than we could imagine. She knew things about him she couldn't tell us, which made her love him even more.

"We tried coaxing her for more information, but she refused and said she probably already had divulged too much. Grandpa never spoke about his childhood other than saying it wasn't happy. We never knew our great-grandparents. Maybe there is something in his past, but murdering Noah? I'm not buying it."

CHAPTER 72

It was a slow day at the Lighthouse Cove police station. While Ed and Brad were in Rochester, Carrie finally had time to look through cold case files to see if she could locate the one for the young reporter who had been murdered 25 years ago. She asked Mia to help; in less than an hour they found it.

Ed had remembered correctly. Kate Stone, age 27, had been physically assaulted and then tossed into the water where she drowned, her body found on the beach at Chimney Bluffs. A reporter for the *Silver Bay Times*, she wrote general news stories and features; her editor had informed the police that there was nothing controversial about any of them.

Shortly before her death, she had written a story about Desmond Kane, related to the expansion of Kane Global Transport. He was a person of interest but they could find no motive, and his alibi checked out. She phoned Ed.

He excused himself and walked into the hallway outside the DA's office to take the call. Carrie reported she'd located the cold case file and told him what she'd learned about Desmond Kane. She wondered if instead of Chris, he might be Noah's killer.

Ed replied, "Yes. Chris just gave us information that could implicate his grandfather. I'll give you the details when we get back."

He walked back into the DA's office. "Did you know your grandfather was questioned about the murder of a young reporter about 25 years ago? Her name was Kate Stone."

He looked shocked. "No, I had no idea."

"He had an alibi; the case went cold, but he was one of the last persons to see her alive."

"Look, we need to get to the bottom of this, Ed. I think you should speak to my grandfather as soon as possible, and I'd like to go with you. I'll clear my calendar for the rest of the day."

Chris called his grandfather and said that he and the two investigators from Lighthouse Cove had questions for him about Noah Pierce's death. His grandfather responded that he would prefer to speak with them at home instead of at the office and could be there in half an hour.

When Chris asked about his grandmother's whereabouts, Desmond replied that she was having an early lunch with some friends at their country club and then playing bridge. She wouldn't be home until later that afternoon.

Ed apologized to Chris for suspecting him. The district attorney said he understood. Given the evidence, it was reasonable for Ed to believe he'd killed Noah Pierce, and there were no hard feelings. He said he hoped the friendship they'd begun would continue, but he felt sick to think that his grandfather may have been responsible for Noah Pierce's death.

Half an hour later, the three men arrived at the Kane home, a lovely, sprawling 1930s-era stone and frame two-story with leaded mullioned windows that looked like something out of a James Stewart movie, on a tree-lined cul-de-sac. They pulled into a driveway that circled around to the back of the house and parked in front of a free-standing three-car garage.

Like his son, Greg, Desmond looked nothing like Chris. He was small and wiry, with straight white hair combed back and the clear, silver-blue eyes that seemed to be a family trait.

Desmond ushered them into the study. He sat in a leather wing chair and motioned for the others to sit on the sofa across from him.

"I think I know why you're here. How did you figure it out?"

Chris said the investigators had a video that showed a car like his picking Noah up early on the morning that he died, and that when Ed and his wife were with them on the boat on Saturday night, Ed found evidence that Noah had been on the trawler. Until that evening, he and Elena hadn't taken the boat out all summer.

"I admit Noah was with me, but I didn't kill him; it was a tragic accident."

Desmond explained that Noah had called to set a time and date to interview him about the piece he was writing about Chris.

"Every so often at the height of my career I'd play hooky and go fishing by myself early in the morning. It was meditative and helped me focus. I know I promised our family that my wife and I wouldn't take the boat out unless one of them was present, but I'm still in pretty good shape and thought it would be fun, perhaps one last time, to go fishing that morning. I asked Noah if he wanted to join me; we could talk and fish at the same time, as long as I was back at work between 10:00 and 10:30.

"Noah liked the idea; he said he fished with his father when he was a kid and they still went out together when he visited his parents in Gananoque. He asked if we could go to Chimney Bluffs.

"When I asked why Chimney Bluffs, he said he was curious; he'd never been there and had heard it was a great fishing spot. At first I hesitated and then thought, '*why not?*' It really didn't

230 MURDER AT CHIMNEY BLUFFS

matter if I was a little late for work that day. There was nothing pressing on my calendar. He didn't have a rod; I said I'd lend him one of mine.

"I picked him up at approximately 5:00 a.m., and we drove to the marina. We made small talk; when we anchored at Chimney Bluffs, he said that the real reason he wanted to speak with me was about something he learned when he was doing research at the library about a fire that killed one of his ancestors near Chimney Bluffs during Prohibition, and if I didn't mind, we could schedule the interview about Chris for another time.

"I had an inkling of what he was referring to, but hoped I was mistaken. He opened his laptop to a file and showed me some newspaper articles and court reports and asked to write a feature story about my life. He thought it would be inspirational to readers. He hadn't told his editor he'd be meeting with me that morning; he didn't want to lie to her about the reason he'd be late to work that day. I couldn't allow him to write that story."

Desmond looked at the investigators and said, "For context, I suppose you should know about a man named Etan Canersky, a murderer, rumrunner, mobster and a master of disguise."

CHAPTER 73

Ed was puzzled about the connection between Desmond Kane and the notorious rumrunner. He had assumed Noah's death had something to do with the newspaper assignment.

Brad turned on his phone's recording device and they listened, intrigued, while Desmond spoke about Canersky's life up until the time he escaped to Chicago, leaving his wife, Phoebe and son, Frank, to fend for themselves in Rochester. Because of Annie's research and their trip to Chicago, Ed knew most of the details, but not what happened to Frank after his father abandoned him and his mother.

As he grew older, Frank was constantly in trouble with the law. He dropped out of high school and connected with the Rochester mob, where he first worked as a bag man, then an enforcer, and finally, after proving his loyalty, a hit man. His mother knew what he was doing, but as with her husband, she looked the other way.

"When he was in his early twenties, Frank met a pretty, young woman, Alice Rossi, at a neighborhood church festival.

Desmond continued. "He was a charming sociopath who told her he was the manager of a restaurant in her neighborhood. She had no idea the business was owned by the local mob boss who provided Frank with a cover to continue his wet work.

"They dated for a year and married. Their only child, Desimo, was born a year after that. Many years later he became Desmond Kane, the man you see before you now."

Chris stared, astounded. Incredulous, Ed asked, "You're Frank's son and Etan Canersky's grandson?"

"I am."

Ed now realized why the elderly man and his son, Greg, looked so familiar to him. They were spitting images of the photos he'd seen of Canersky before he became a master of disguise.

"My father was eventually arrested and convicted of killing a man from a rival mob, repeating the pattern of abandoning his wife and child like my grandfather did. He was murdered in prison six months after he was incarcerated."

Desmond continued, "I was 16 when my mother died of cancer. She, too, was an only child, and her parents died when I was young. I barely remember them. I had no other family to support me; I was all alone. The mobster my father worked for approached me at the funeral and offered me a job. I declined. I had no desire to live a life of crime. Surprisingly, I never heard from him again.

"My mother and I lived in a small rental apartment. She had a little money saved when she died, but that went quickly, and I was forced to find work to support myself and pay the rent while I finished high school. After I graduated, I had difficulty finding employment, given my father's sins. I took whatever odd jobs I could get, driving a cab, delivering furniture, but I struggled to make ends meet.

"I missed my gentle, loving mother, and was furious that my father had abandoned us. Despite my pledge not to follow in my grandfather's or father's footsteps, I got in with the wrong crowd, and one day did something stupid. I participated in the armed robbery of a neighborhood grocery store. The others escaped; I got caught, and as a first offender, was sentenced to five years in jail.

"Then my luck began to change. The judge who sentenced me saw something in me that made him believe I was salvageable. He frequently visited me while I was incarcerated, and after I was out, took me under his wing. I was homeless by then, and the judge let me stay in the carriage house on his property until I got back on my feet.

"I knew I needed to put my past behind me and asked for his advice. He suggested I change my name; the son of a notorious murderer and grandson of another would not have an easy time finding employment, especially since I also had a criminal record.

"The judge secured a new social security number for me and a driver's license. I don't know how he was able to do that; he always struck me as a 'by the books' man.

"A childhood friend of his owned a trucking company and hired me as a long-distance driver. I worked my way up to management and many years later bought and expanded the company, now known as Kane Global Transport.

"I had never been religious but when I was driving I started attending church, and that's where I met and eventually married Mary Elizabeth, whose father was the vicar. She and her family knew about my past but because of their strong religious beliefs, forgave me. I never broke the law again."

"Grandpa, I don't understand why you never said anything about this to us. You have nothing to be ashamed of. You completely turned your life around. Not many people would have been able to accomplish what you did, given your family's history."

"Chris, I wanted to leave the past behind. Only the judge, his family, your grandmother and her parents knew about my less-than-stellar beginnings. I believed my secret was safe. That is, until Noah Pierce came along."

Desmond said, "I was shocked. I thought the judge had expunged my criminal record. Apparently, I was wrong. He either missed that detail or changed his mind at the last minute, should my upward trajectory turn into a downward spiral again.

"Noah told me about his quest to find out what happened to an ancestor who drowned trying to escape being burned to death. But then, curious about what happened after my grandfather escaped, he continued his research and followed a trail that led him to me.

"He was fascinated and asked to write a feature story about my life. He said readers would be inspired by my ability to rise above my family's shady past to become a pillar of the community. The reason I refused is that I am, and will always be, ashamed of that past, and other than the few people I mentioned, I decided long ago that no one else would ever know the truth."

CHAPTER 74

Desmond said, "Chris, you're considering running for attorney general. The media would have a field day if they learned about Etan and Frank; you know how they can distort things. I was afraid that someone would assume, because of my background, that my business dealings were shady and insinuate that my children and grandchildren were involved. I couldn't let that happen."

"We could have weathered the storm, Grandpa. We have plenty of resources to counter bad publicity. I love you, and what you've done with your life since your childhood would be inspirational to so many people whose lives began the way yours did. How did Noah react when you said you didn't want him to write the story?"

"Incredibly, he didn't try to convince me to change my mind. When I explained, he said my secret was safe with him. He'd stick with his original plan to write the profile about you with my comments, and the story about the fire as a feature for the newspaper, ending with Etan's escape to Chicago. I trusted him to keep his word. He was a truly exceptional young man, and I will regret his death for the rest of my days."

"What happened next?" Ed asked.

He wiped his eyes. "With the interview completed, Noah grabbed a rod and started fishing from the cockpit when the wind picked up and high waves rocked the boat. I was in the cabin at the time, and when I realized what was happening, became alarmed and shouted for him to come inside.

"He had just pulled the rod out of the water when the boat lurched, and he fell back and hit his head against the steps going to upper deck. He stood up and steadied himself against the railing.

"I noticed a gash on his head. I led him inside, got the first aid kit out and put pressure on the wound until it stopped bleeding, but there were no bandages large enough in the kit. He said he had a bad headache and felt dizzy and sick. I feared he had a concussion.

"The wind was still fierce. I hoped if I were careful I could make it back to Lighthouse Cove to get medical treatment for him. I wanted to call ahead so the first responders would be waiting for us, but remembered I'd left my cell phone in the car, and unfortunately, when I tried it, the radio was broken.

"I went back outside to see if there were any boats nearby that I could flag down, but most had started toward shore when they realized a storm was brewing. Noah followed me saying he had his phone and started to pull it out of his pocket when another wave rocked the boat.

"The impact was strong; Noah dropped his phone onto the swim platform. I said for him to let it go; it wasn't safe to try to retrieve it. He didn't listen. He opened the gate as another wave hit and fell onto the platform.

"I reached over and shouted for him to grab my hand; instead, when he stood up still dizzy, he fell into the water. I grabbed a life preserver and threw it to him, but it slipped from his grasp, and he disappeared."

"You promised you wouldn't go out on a boat without someone from the family who could assist if you ran into difficulty, Grandpa. You didn't listen, and as a result a young man is dead. You could have died, too. What you did is reprehensible."

Desmond was silent for a moment then said, "I know what I promised, but I didn't think one more time would make a difference. I was sure I could handle it, and when we left Irondequoit the forecast was for smooth sailing. I never meant for any of this to happen."

"What did you do with Noah's laptop?" Ed asked.

Desmond said he tossed it into the water. "I had no intention of reporting the accident. What difference would it make? It wouldn't bring him back, and I wanted to avoid a scandal. It didn't make sense to hold onto it."

"Didn't you notice his coffee mug?" Ed asked.

"I remember the mug; he'd left it on the counter when he went outside to fish. I didn't think to look for it. I was concentrating on getting rid of the laptop and then getting the boat safely back to Irondequoit. Ed, I know you were on the trawler on Saturday night. Where did you find it?"

"It must have fallen off the countertop and under a bench when the wave rocked the boat. I found it when I tripped over the threshold and bent to tie my shoe."

CHAPTER 75

Chris said, "When you called me back the morning Noah died, you said you were in your office, but that's not true is it? I was hearing boat blasts, not truck horns; you were just leaving the marina, weren't you?"

Desmond hung his head and mumbled, "I'm sorry I lied to you. I hope you can believe that it's the first time. I hope you can forgive me."

"Does Grandma know about what happened? One night when you and dad were away on a business trip with mom, Elena and I took her to dinner. We asked about the secret to your strong relationship, she said one of the reasons is that you were always completely honest with each other."

"No, not this time. She would have urged me to come forward with the truth. I hope she'll forgive me and we can weather this storm, we've been married for such a long time, and I love her dearly."

Brad said, "I don't know how much you know about technology, but didn't you think Noah had a backup file somewhere? You still could have been implicated in his death."

"I know a little. Even if someone found a backup file and read about my past, I wouldn't have been implicated in his death if there was no proof he'd been on the boat with me. Remember, he hadn't told anyone about our meeting."

Normally calm and reasonable, Ed felt anger begin to simmer.

He asked, "Did you ever consider that Noah's body might have never washed up on the beach and his family would have always wondered what happened to him? What if it got caught up in rocks or seaweed, or drifted out further into the lake? "

"As I just said, the lake was choppy that morning and the waves were strong. I was positive his body would eventually be found."

Desmond shook his head. "All that mattered to me, *matters* to me, is my family. My grandfather was a murderer who abandoned his wife and son, my father did the same thing to me and my mother.

"I vowed that if I ever married and had my own family, I would change that pattern. That's why I didn't report what happened, and that's why I didn't want Noah to write the story. I would never let them suffer the way I did. Protecting them from learning the truth about me and what happened was for them, not me."

Ed rolled his eyes and shook his head.

Chris said, "Ed, as outraged as I am about what happened, I believe my grandfather. If you remember, I mentioned on Saturday night that we'd been having problems with the radio and that a life preserver was missing, which verifies Grandpa's story."

Quiet during the entire exchange, Brad muttered, "Doesn't prove a thing. You could be protecting him."

Chris glared at him. "But I'm not."

He walked over to his grandfather and looked him straight in the eyes. "I believe you when you say Noah's death was an accident but taking the boat out by yourself when you were explicitly asked not to and then not reporting Noah's death is unforgivable."

Ed said, "You're not off the hook, Desmond. Even if the DA believes your story, it's likely you'll be charged with obstruction of justice for lying to me about your whereabouts the morning Noah died, and possibly for destroying evidence."

The elderly man remained silent.

He continued. "There's something else we need to address. Twenty-five years ago, you were questioned about the murder of a young female reporter named Kate Stone, who was physically assaulted and dumped in the water near Chimney Bluffs where she drowned. She interviewed you when you started to expand your company.

"Did she also learn about your past, but unlike Noah, wasn't willing to bury the story? There's no statute of limitations on murder, so if you killed her and we can prove it, you will be charged and go to trial."

Desmond said, "Absolutely not. Yes, I was questioned then, but if you read about the case you'll know I had an ironclad alibi with witnesses. I didn't murder Noah, and I didn't murder that young lady. That she died in a similar fashion is purely coincidental."

CHAPTER 76

Chris stayed inside with his grandfather while the investigators went outside to talk.

"Ed, are you buying this?" Brad asked. "He could just be a fabulous liar."

"He could be, but his explanation certainly sounds plausible. I expect the DA will believe him. He's led a stellar life, no evidence of any scandals, and what happened could be a terrible lapse in judgement. At his age it would be no surprise.

"And remember, Mike never said Noah was murdered, just that the death seemed suspicious and it was up to us to find out what happened to him.

"Even if he's telling the truth about the accident, he lied about the phone calls and his whereabouts the morning Noah died. As I said to him, he's probably facing obstruction charges, and possibly charges for destroying evidence. Our DA will be the one to decide. We should get back inside."

"I'm going to stay here for a few minutes, Ed. I want to call Carrie with an update."

Brad placed the call. Carrie put him on hold and called Sean O'Leary, the Wayne County district attorney, on her office phone. A few minutes later, she got back on the line and told

Brad to bring Desmond in. He'd be charged with obstruction of justice, but a murder charge was off the table.

"And what about charging him with destroying evidence?"

"That's off the table, too. It would be difficult to prove there was anything in the missing laptop that could tie Desmond to Noah's death. I really wish we could also charge him with failure to report an accident, but as you know, in New York that's not a crime."

He went back into the house, Mirandized and arrested Desmond.

Chris said, "Grandpa, as disgusted as I am about what you did, you need an attorney. I'm going to call Garrett Rosenfeld and ask him to represent you."

Chris called his friend, who said he'd meet Desmond at the Lighthouse Cove police station in 45 minutes.

"He's on his way Grandpa. Don't say a word until he gets there."

He shook his head. "I can't believe this is happening. I'm going home to tell Elena; after that, we'll go to the club to get Grandma and let her know that Grandpa's been arrested."

CHAPTER 77

They sat him in a small interview room waiting for Garrett, who arrived several minutes later.

Carrie called the DA. "Sean, I'm still a bit skeptical that Desmond Kane is telling the truth. Are you certain you can't charge him with murder?"

"I am, Carrie. With his reputation and no proof that what happened to Noah Pierce wasn't an accident, no jury will find him guilty.

"We'll stick with the obstruction of justice charge. There's plenty of evidence to prove that: his confession, the phone conversation with his grandson, and his initial conversation with Ed when he lied about his whereabouts the morning of Noah's death."

"Will he serve prison time?"

"It's a Class A misdemeanor with punishment of a year in prison or up to three years' probation, so, yes, that could happen, but I expect the judge will grant leniency if he takes a plea deal."

They left the police station and transported Desmond to the courthouse for arraignment. Garrett pulled the DA aside and asked him to drop the charges.

"Sean, he admitted what happened, he's not likely to commit any more crimes, he's no danger to society, and at his age I think his family will keep a very close eye on him after this."

He said, "I can't do it, Garrett. Noah's family believed their son was murdered, and if Desmond had come forward earlier, the case could have been closed and they could have been mourning his death as a tragic accident.

"What I will do, if he agrees to waive a trial and plead guilty, is request that instead of jail time he get probation, perhaps instead of three years the judge will agree to two, given his age, reputation and standing in the community. Give me a minute, I'll call him."

Shortly after, Sean gave Garrett a thumbs up. "Admission of guilt, and two years."

"I'll speak with him. I expect he'll take the deal."

Desmond pleaded guilty of obstruction of justice and was released on his own recognizance. Despite the DA's recommendation, the judge refused to confiscate his passport, indicating that he had no reason to believe the elderly man would be a flight risk over so minor a charge.

Mary Elizabeth Kane was sitting on a sofa in the study with Chris and Elena when her husband arrived home. She turned her head to the side when he bent down to kiss her and refused to speak to him.

Later that evening during dinner, Ed told Annie about Desmond Kane's involvement in Noah's death and his subsequent arrest. He reminded her of their conversation the night Andy Spurling showed them the speakeasy, and that as usual her instincts were spot on.

The young reporter's death had been related, in an obscure way, to what happened to his ancestor and the proprietor of

Tony's Place, but neither of them could have ever imagined that the philanthropic octogenarian would be in the center of it all and inadvertently been responsible for the tragedy.

She said she wasn't surprised; it made sense given the circumstances. Then something else struck her. She had always wondered why Terri was so attracted to men who worked in law enforcement and now thought she had an answer. It might have been her experience with Chris when she was barely an adult, a man who believed in her and gave her a chance to straighten out her life.

"Ed, as much as I've always liked Terri, I'm disappointed and somewhat angry that she lied to Elena about how she knew Chris, even if it was, as I suspect, because she was ashamed to talk about it in front of me. I wouldn't have judged her, and I'm more than peeved that she caused my new friend so much distress. I have to think about whether I can let it go or confront her about it."

"I'd let it go, Annie. You and Terri are friendly but not friends, and it's really none of your business. It would be more appropriate for Chris to speak with her, although my guess is that he won't. He has enough on his plate dealing with family issues right now.

"You're right, of course, although I am going to have a much harder time being cordial to her when I'm at the Bistro."

CHAPTER 78

Despite efforts to keep the press from learning about what happened, a reporter who monitored police and court reports obtained the information. The day after Desmond's arrest and arraignment, it was the headline story for the *Rochester Daily News* and *Silver Bay Times.*

A broken man, Desmond became reclusive and refused to leave his home. Furious with him, Mary Elizabeth traveled to Arizona for an extended visit with her sister, but eventually returned and forgave him; he had been a kind, faithful and loving husband throughout their long marriage. His relationship with Chris, who keenly felt the pain of his betrayal, was never quite the same.

Public support for Chris endured despite the scandal, and he was encouraged to run for attorney general. Instead, he resigned as the Monroe County district attorney. He believed an opponent would have a field day with his family's history; he didn't want the controversy to touch his wife and children.

Chris' father offered him a position in the legal department of KGT, but he wasn't interested in doing corporate work. By fall, he was teaching criminal law at the University of Rochester, which gave him more time to be with his family and to support Elena's burgeoning career as an artist.

The summer gathering with Suzanne, Garrett and the Kanes at the DeCleryk's house had never materialized for obvious reasons, but there were no hard feelings and a few months later, Elena invited Ed and Annie to view her exhibit at the grand opening of Jon Bradford's expansion of Gallery 21.

Later that evening, the DeCleryks, and Suzanne and Garrett hosted a small celebratory dinner party for Elena at a café within walking distance from the gallery. They avoided speaking about the case until Chris brought it up.

He said his grandfather had recently been diagnosed with dementia. His grandparents had sold their home and would be moving into a continuing care facility. He admitted he was still struggling with what his grandfather had done and reiterated that he felt no anger toward Ed; he knew he was only doing his job.

CHAPTER 79

Noah's family, while relieved their son's death had most likely been accidental, was furious that Desmond Kane hadn't come forward to report it. They had no choice but to accept the DA's decision to give the man probation instead of jail time but were disappointed that the crime hadn't resulted in a stiffer penalty.

Ed continued to believe that somewhere in the young journalist's possessions there had to be a list of his usernames and passwords. He had an idea and reached for his phone.

"Hi, Brad. It's Ed. I've been thinking about the box Noah's medal was in. Do you remember what it looked like?"

"I do. Why?"

"I'll get to that in a minute. Was the lining flat or puffy?"

"Puffy, like the inside of a ring box, but without the slit for the ring. What's this about?"

He explained. Brad called the Pierces and said he'd wait on the phone while they looked under the lining of the box.

"It's here!" Sam Pierce said. "I can't believe it. What would you like me to do with it?" They had found a small, folded piece of paper with a printed list of Noah's passwords and usernames.

Brad called Ed. "You were spot on. They're scanning and emailing the list to both of us. I'm in the middle of something right now. Would you mind going into the Cloud to see what the files on his laptop contain and let me know what you find?"

Ed called Brad back an hour later. He had been able to open all the files and reported that everything was there: the notes with Noah's research on the fire that killed his ancestor, copies of newspaper articles about Etan Canersky, and the information he learned about Desmond Kane's past.

Brad said, "Brilliant idea, Ed."

"Thanks, but if I'd thought about where he might have hidden the list weeks ago, the case would have been solved much earlier. I must be losing my touch."

"Ed, you have no reason to blame yourself. You were with Carol Smalley when we conducted the search in Noah's apartment. Before we handed it over to the Pierces, we should have lifted the lining to see if anything was under it. This isn't on you; we were the ones who dropped the ball. At least now the family has some closure."

Ed said, "I'm still perplexed about why Desmond tried to hide the accident that killed Noah. If he had told the truth in the beginning, I'm certain his reputation would have been salvaged and Chris might have been elected as the next attorney general."

CHAPTER 80

The crazy summer season ended with a series of concerts, craft fairs, and fireworks on the bluff during the Labor Day holiday weekend. Ed, now relaxed and with time for reflection, admitted to Annie that he wasn't quite ready to retire and hoped to work at least one or two more cases. She wasn't surprised and supported his decision.

One evening two weeks later, she received a call from Suzanne inviting her and Ed to join her, Garrett, Sheila and Amy, for dinner at Rumrunners that Saturday night.

"Ed, she said they have exciting news to share."

"You don't think…."

"They're expecting a baby?" She laughed. "Of course not. Remember, they're both in their 50s, and his boys from his previous marriage are young adults. I guess we'll have to wait until we see them to find out what this is all about.

"You know what? Instead of meeting at Rumrunners, let's invite them here. The weather is gorgeous, and you know I love to cook when I have the time. We could eat on the porch and watch the sunset."

"That's a great idea. Let's do it."

Annie called their friends who didn't want to put the DeCleryks to any trouble, but when she insisted, they relented.

Annie started cooking the morning of the party. She prepared the pomegranate and orange glaze for the pork loin, a tomato salad with basil vinaigrette, corn salad, and assembled the dessert—peach bread pudding—that she'd bake while they were having hors d'œuvres.

In the meantime, Ed placed wood in the grate of the stone fireplace on the porch should the evening turn cool. After that, he set the table with a French Provençal tablecloth and napkins, white ceramic dishes, colorful wine and water glasses, and for the centerpiece, a huge vase of sunflowers from their garden.

Everyone had dressed festively for the occasion: the women in flowing pants and pastel-colored tops and the men in slacks and silk shirts. They laughed when they saw each other.

"Apparently everyone got the memo," Annie remarked, smiling.

The group talked amiably over wine and hors d'oeuvres, sitting in Adirondack chairs set in a circle on the lawn. Garrett reported that there was a scandal brewing at the office where Peyton Stewart's father worked as a stockbroker. Reilly Logan, the COO, had been arrested on drug charges; he'd been the supplier the young drug dealer had refused to identify because the man had threatened to kill his family if he ever revealed Logan's name.

Garrett had been asked to represent the man but declined; he didn't want to have anything to do with someone involved in the drug trade. A judge was reviewing Peyton's case, and rumor had it she was considering shortening his sentence, given the extenuating circumstances.

When they sat down for dinner. Annie looked at Suzanne and said, "You wanted to share some news with us, and here we are waiting with bated breath. Do we have to withhold your food from you until you tell us what it is?"

CHAPTER 81

Suzanne laughed and glanced at her husband. "It's not my story. Honey, how about if you tell our good friends what's going on?"

Garrett grinned. "Sorry to keep you in suspense. Sheila and I are leaving the law firm in Rochester and establishing our own general practice in Lighthouse Cove."

"Wow! What precipitated this?" Ed asked.

He responded, "Partially agreeing to represent Desmond Kane. I'm disgusted about what he did, and being asked to defend Reilly Logan was the last straw."

Sheila said, "I've been feeling the same way. My last several cases have soured me on continuing as a defense attorney."

Annie pumped a fist. "That's great news! Are you moving here or going to be commuting from Rochester? Have you found office space?"

The attorneys had just closed on purchasing the historic building across from the post office that had originally been an inn, but in recent years had been turned into a restaurant with several unused rooms on the second floor. They'd renovate the first floor for their offices, and the second into living space for Sheila and Amy until they found a permanent home in the village; after that they'd rent it out.

Annie remarked that secrets were hard to keep in the village; she was surprised no one had heard about it, and they had no idea the building had been for sale.

"We heard about the sale from another partner in the firm who deals with real estate transactions and said the owner was a client. We jumped on it and advised the real estate agent that if the word got out, the deal wouldn't occur. She apparently believed us." Garrett grinned.

"What about your homes in Rochester?" Ed asked.

"At first we considered keeping ours as an investment property but ultimately decided to sell it." Sheila answered. "We wanted to be closer to the water and have always wanted to live here."

"I'll be moving into the cottage here full time. I've sold the condo to the young attorney who will be replacing me," Garrett said.

"Amy, are you still going to be working as the pastry chef for Callaloo?" Ed asked.

"No. I have some news, too. I'll be running the bakery side of the business for Louise from the building she recently bought that's next door."

Ed responded, "When I stopped in several weeks ago to purchase coffee and muffins, she was pretty frazzled, which is very unlike her. She confessed she's overwhelmed and was hoping to find a partner who could run the bakery for her.

"I thought about you but figured since you lived and worked in Rochester and seemed blissfully happy as Callaloo's pastry chef, you wouldn't be interested, so I didn't mention it."

"It was serendipitous. Sheila and I were there for lunch one day and Louise said the same thing to me, then asked if I'd be interested in working with her. Sheila and Garrett had already decided to open a practice here. I jumped at the opportunity."

"Amy, how did Suzanne's parents react when they learned you were leaving?" Annie asked.

"They were fine with it. Suzanne can tell you about it."

Suzanne responded, "It was perfect timing. My parents are in their 70s and have been thinking about retiring, but they decided to wait until the right buyer came along.

"My cousin and her husband run a bakery in Brooklyn, but they've always wanted to open a restaurant. My parents persuaded them to sell, move up here, run their bakery, and work side-by-side with them to learn the restaurant business. If things work out, they'll buy it from them in a year or two."

Ed smiled. "I couldn't begin to figure out what it was you wanted to tell us, but it's fabulous news. Now we'll be able to spend even more time with all of you."

EPILOGUE

July, a year later

On a bright, warm day, shortly after Annie returned to her office after giving a tour of the Prohibition exhibit to a group of Canadians from Kingston, Ontario, her phone rang.

She looked at the caller ID. It was Andy Spurling, who had recently been elected to serve on her board of directors.

"Good morning, Andy. It's a lovely day. How are you?"

"I'm well. What about you?"

"Me, too. But I'm glad the weekend is over; now I can take a bit of a breather.

"What can I do for you?"

"I have another surprise for you. When you have a chance can you stop by? Ed's welcome to come along."

"Would today before lunch work?"

"It would."

"Ed won't be with me. He's in Ithaca today, teaching a class at Cornell on murder investigations for his friend, Samir Abadi. They met as Navy SEALs, but Samir went on to work as an analyst for the CIA and after he retired, was hired as a professor in the graduate school of government there. What's going on?

Did you find another speakeasy? You've certainly piqued my curiosity."

Andy laughed. "No, no speakeasies, but you're going to like it."

"I'll be there in fifteen minutes."

A short while later, Annie sat in Andy's office while he explained that he and his wife had recently purchased the land across the inlet from the restaurant.

"We've been interested in it for years. You can see from here that it's completely overgrown with reeds, tall sea grasses and brambles, but it faces the water and is a perfect site for a small bed and breakfast. Our plan is to eventually construct a walking bridge for our guests across the inlet to the restaurant."

"What a great idea. Who sold it to you?"

"That was the challenge. When our attorney searched for a title to the property, he couldn't find an owner; it had been vacant for a hundred years. Since no taxes had been paid, the municipality assumed possession. Anyway, long story short, they agreed to sell it to us; in fact, they were delighted to have it back on the tax rolls. I'll take you there now."

He drove from the restaurant's parking lot to the main road and then made an immediate left turn onto a dirt driveway that led to a small promontory that overlooked the lake. Nestled in a thicket of tangled trees and bushes stood a large crumbling barn with a caving roof; in front of it was a small, decrepit house smothered with vines, and beside it mostly submerged in the water, a rotting boathouse.

They got out of the car and walked around the property. Annie was amazed.

"Andy, did you have any idea these buildings were here before you decided to purchase the land?"

"None. It was a complete surprise; I thought it was just an empty parcel of land. We've received all the permits we need to start the project. We're going to tear everything down and clear the land, but before we do, I want to show you something."

He escorted her to the barn. "Be very careful," Andy said, as he opened the barn-door. "Some of the floorboards are rotting, and as you can see, the roof isn't in great shape."

He offered his hand, and she stepped inside. A couple of large blue tarps lay atop what appeared to be a boat. Andy removed them and set them aside.

"Oh my, is that a shadow boat?"

"It is. Care to guess who it belonged to?"

"Etan Canersky?"

"Not exactly; it belonged to someone else before."

"Liam O'Connor? I guess I assumed Canersky destroyed that boat after he escaped and that this is one he purchased later."

Andy guided Annie around to the side of the boat. "Instead of destroying it, Canersky painted over the boat's original name, *Whyte Wytch*, and renamed it *Grey Goose*. I expect he continued to use it for his rumrunning business the entire time he operated the speakeasy next door.

"The original name was bleeding through. A restoration specialist removed the overlaid paint. We also found O'Connor's name engraved in the cockpit under the steering wheel."

"I'm surprised Canersky didn't find a way to destroy the engraving."

"That wouldn't have been easy. He probably didn't think anyone would notice and perhaps it gave him satisfaction every time he saw it to know that he'd stolen the boat from O'Connor."

"What about the house? Do you have any evidence that Canersky lived in it with his family when he was running the speakeasy?"

"We think so. We unearthed some old newspaper articles hidden in a trunk that date back to the time he escaped, some of the same ones you showed the board that you found at the library."

"I must admit, I never expected this. What will you do with it?"

"That's the surprise. It's yours. For the museum. A gift."

"Andy, that's so very generous, but we have no place for it."

"I know. I spoke with Bill Ronson, who owns the antique boat museum a few miles down on Rt. 14. He's agreed to display the boat; it will be on permanent loan from the historical society. In exchange, all he'd like you to do is to help him promote his museum by carrying his brochures."

"With pleasure. I'll call and thank him. We'll have a photo taken of the boat, frame it and hang it on a wall in the hall before you enter the speakeasy. We'll place a QR code under the photo that will give our guests information about the boat and its history, with a note that they can see the original at the boat museum."

She reached up and hugged the restaurateur. "Thanks so very much. I can't wait to tell Ed about this. Oh, by the way, at the next board meeting I'm going to ask for approval to name the space *The Noah Pierce Memorial Exhibit Gallery*."

"I can't imagine anyone having a problem with that. It's a nice tribute; I expect his parents will be delighted. If it weren't for him, you never would have gone to the library in the first place and learned the history about the fire and Tony's Place."

Later that afternoon, Annie set a table with cheese, crackers and a bottle of wine on the porch. When Ed arrived home, she poured them each a glass and excitedly announced Andy's discovery of Liam O'Connor's boat.

"We've come full circle, Ed. Murders on the lake, secrets and lies, and a hundred years later the case is closed. I'm just sorry Noah didn't live long enough to see it."

ANNIE'S RECIPES

PROVENÇAL TUNA SANDWICHES

- ½ C. red wine vinegar
- 6 anchovy fillets, rinsed, patted dry and minced
- 2 garlic cloves, minced
- 1 C. extra-virgin olive oil
- 2 (8-inch) round loves crusty bread
- 2 C. thinly sliced radishes
- 2 C. loosely packed basil leaves
- 1 C. minced onion, soaked in cold water for 10 min. and well drained
- 2 (6 ½ oz.) cans tuna in oil, drained and flaked
- 4 ripe tomatoes (about 1 ½ pounds)

In a bowl, whisk together vinegar, anchovies, garlic, salt and pepper to taste. Add oil in a stream, whisking until emulsified. Halve the breads horizontally and hollow out halves, leaving ½ inch thick shells. Spoon one fourth of dressing evenly into each half. Working with one loaf at a time, arrange half of radish in one bottom shell and top with one fourth of basil. Sprinkle half of onion over basil. Arrange half of tuna on onion and top with one third of remaining basil. Arrange half of tomatoes on basil and fit top shell over tomatoes. Assemble second sandwich in the same manner. Wrap sandwiches in plastic wrap and put in a shallow baking pan. Top sandwiches with a second baking sheet and weight down with several pounds of weight to compress sandwiches. Chill one hour. Sandwiches may be made up to 4 hours ahead. Serve chilled sandwiches cut into wedges.
Serves six.

RED BELL PEPPER DIP

- 1 small red onion, quartered
- 1 T. olive oil
- 1 (7-oz.) jar roasted red bell peppers, drained
- 12 fresh basil leaves or ½ tsp. dried
- 12 oz. cream cheese room temperature

Preheat oven to 400 degrees. Place onion in small baking dish and drizzle olive oil over. Bake until soft, 35–45 minutes. Cool.

Puree onion with roasted bell peppers and basil in food processor. Add cream cheese and blend until combined. Transfer to bowl, cover and refrigerate and serve with pita chips, chilled cooked asparagus, cherry tomatoes, mushrooms. Makes 2.5 cups Serves six.

SEAFOOD QUICHE

- Store bought pastry crust for a two-crust pie

Filling:
- 1 ½ T. butter
- ¼ C. minced red onion
- ½ lb. medium uncooked shrimp, peeled and deveined
- ⅓ lb. bay scallops, connective tissue removed
- 1 C. cooked crabmeat
- 1 C. whipping cream
- ½ C. milk
- ½ C. fresh Italian parsley
- 1 tsp. minced fresh tarragon or ¼ tsp. dried
- 3 large eggs

- 2 egg yolks
- 1 tsp. grated lemon peel
- 1 tsp. salt
- ¼ tsp. pepper
- 1 ¼ C. packed grated Monterey Jack Cheese
  (about 5 ounces)

Allow crusts to come to room temperature and then piece them together and roll out to a 15x12 rectangle. Gently transfer to 12x 7.5 x 1.5 baking dish (you can also use a 9x13, but the crust will be a little thinner). Freeze crust for 15 minutes, then line with pie weights or dried beans and bake at 375 degrees until sides are set, and crust is golden brown (about 15 minutes.) Crust can be prepared one day in advance and stored at room temperature.

Preheat oven to 375 degrees. Melt butter in heavy skillet over medium heat. Add minced red onion and sauté for three minutes. Add shrimp and scallops and sauté for two minutes. Mix in crab meat. Transfer seafood mixture to a colander and let drain. While draining, whisk cream, milk, parsley, tarragon, eggs, grated lemon peel, salt and pepper in a large bowl to blend. Mix in seafood mixture and cheese.

Ladle filling into crust. Bake until custard is set, about 45 minutes. Cool for 20 minutes and cut into squares.
Serves six to eight.

MIXED GREENS & MUSHROOM SALAD

- 5 T. Balsamic vinegar
- 1 T. Dijon mustard
- ½ tsp. dried thyme
- ⅔ C. olive oil

- ¾ pound mushrooms quartered

Cut into small pieces:
- 1 head radicchio
- 2 heads Belgian endive
- 1 head curly endive
- Slice ½ small onion, ½ bunch of fresh chives into small pieces.

Preheat oven to 450 degrees

Whisk vinegar, mustard and oil into a bowl, season to taste with salt and pepper. Place mushrooms on baking sheet, pour ¼ dressing over and toss to coat. Bake until mushrooms are crisp at edges, about 15 minutes. Cool.

Combine mushroom, lettuce, onion and chives in bowl. Add enough dressing to season and toss.

Serves eight.

POUND CAKE WITH STRAWBERRY SAUCE & CHANTILLY CREAM

- 3 C. hulled fresh strawberries
- 6 T. crème de cassis
- 4 T. sugar
- 1 C. chilled whipping cream
- 1 tsp. vanilla extract
- 1 (12-oz.) store bought pound cake, cut into ½ inch thick slices
- 2 pints strawberries, hulled and sliced.

Puree three cups berries with cassis and 2 T. sugar in processor. Strain in sieve to remove seeds. Cover and refrigerate until well-chilled up to one day ahead.

Using an electric mixer, whip cream, remaining 2 T. sugar and vanilla in bowl until soft peaks form. Can be stored covered, and chilled, for up to four hours.

Arrange cake slices on plates, top with sliced berries, spoon strawberry sauce over top. Top with whipped cream.
Serves eight.

PORK LOIN WITH POMEGRANATE & ORANGE GLAZE

- 1 boneless pork loin, about 3 lb., or three small tenderloins, about 1 pound each.

For the Spice Paste:
- 2 tsp. minced garlic
- 2 T. Dijon mustard
- Finely grated zest of one orange
- ⅓ C. orange juice
- 2 T. grated, peeled fresh ginger
- 2 T. pomegranate molasses
- 2 T. soy sauce or coconut aminos

Make the spice paste, rub onto meat and cover and marinate for at least six hours or overnight in refrigerator. Bring to room temperature before cooking.

For the Basting Sauce:
- ⅓ C. orange juice
- 3 T. honey
- 3 T. pomegranate molasses

- 2 T. soy sauce or coconut aminos.

Whisk all ingredients in a small bowl until combined.

Prepare grill. Place pork on grill rack and cook for 15-20 minutes on each side for the large loin and 5 minutes per side for the tenderloins, basting frequently until a nice glaze has formed. Pork should register 140 degrees when finished.

Transfer pork to a cutting board and cover with foil to rest for 8-10 minutes. Slice and Serve.

To roast the meat, cook in a 400-degree oven for at least an hour if using a pork loin, less for tenderloins. Serve remaining basting sauce on side.
Serves six to eight.

TOMATO SALAD WITH BASIL HONEY VINAIGRETTE

- ½ C. chopped fresh basil
- 2 (2 ½ lbs.) flavorful tomatoes of your choice.

For vinaigrette:
- Mix together 3-4 T. balsamic vinegar, 3 T. honey, 1 tsp. salt, ¾ C. extra virgin olive oil

Whisk vinaigrette in small bowl, slice tomatoes, arrange on a platter and drizzle vinaigrette over and serve.
Serves six to eight.

CORN SALAD

- 3 cups frozen corn, defrosted, or six ears fresh corn, shucked with silk rubbed off.

- ½ C. extra virgin olive oil
- 1 C. minced red onion
- 2 tsp. chili powder
- 1 tsp. ground cumin
- 1 red bell pepper, seeded and cut into small dice
- 1 green bell pepper, seeded, and cut into small dice
- 1 ½ C. seeded, diced tomatoes
- 4 T. chopped fresh cilantro
- 3 T. sherry or white balsamic vinegar

Cook corn if not frozen until it is crisp, remove from heat and immerse in cold water to stop the cooking. Drain and pat dry.

In a small fry pan warm ¼ C. olive oil, add the onion and sauté for a few minutes. Add the seasonings and spices, and sauté for another minute.

Combine vegetables in a bowl to mix, add cilantro, remaining olive oil and vinegar and toss well to combine. Season to taste with salt and pepper.
Serves six.

PEACH BREAD PUDDING

- 2 T. butter
- 1 challah, torn into small pieces
- 5 peaches, cut into large chunks
- 4 eggs
- ¾ C. sugar
- 2 C. cream
- ¼ tsp. salt
- ½ tsp. almond extract

Preheat oven to 350°F.

Take ½ T. of the butter and grease a 9" x 9" Pyrex baking dish. Set aside.

Whisk eggs and sugar in a large bowl. Set aside.

Heat the remaining 1½ T. butter over medium heat and add peaches.

Cook about 5 minutes then add cream and mix. Turn off and remove from heat. Quickly add the egg and sugar mixture, almond extract, and salt.

Put the challah into the dish and pour the liquids over. Mix it all up. Bake for 40 minutes covered. Uncover and bake for 15 minutes more or until golden brown

Serves six to eight large portions.

ACKNOWLEDGEMENTS

As the author of the Edmund DeCleryk cozy mysteries, I couldn't have written any of the books without the help of an incredible group of family, friends, beta readers and others who have willingly provided their expertise, technical support and encouragement.

The creation of *Murder at Chimney Bluffs* was in part, a family affair. Since they're all avid readers, I asked my husband, Lyle; my sister, Marcy Brody, and my brother, Alan Green, to serve as my readers. They took hold of the book and provided good suggestions and input that helped smooth out the rough edges.

Thanks, too, to author Patricia Rockwell for reading and reviewing the book, and for the excellent blurb on the back cover. I'd be remiss in not thanking my designer, Celia, at Book Shine Design. As with the others in the series, the cover is marvelous and the book truly does shine as the result of her creativity.

I also want to thank our friends Joe Vater, who shared his expertise about boats, and Jay Maitland, who answered many questions about the criminal justice system.

Each book in the series has a historical backstory that provides clues that help our sleuth solve the crime. I strive to make those details as accurate as possible, albeit with a little creative license, and appreciate the treasure-trove of information available at The Sodus Bay Historical Society and Museum and Sodus Point Village websites. Any errors are mine.

ABOUT THE AUTHOR

Karen Shughart is the author of the award-winning Edmund DeCleryk cozy mystery series, featuring the retired police chief turned criminal consultant and his intrepid wife, Annie, head of the Lighthouse Cove Historical Society, who often steps in to help him solve the crime.

She also has collaborated with other authors on two mysteries and written two non-fiction books. Her books are available in all formats at Amazon, Barnes and Noble, brick and mortar bookshops and gift shops.

She and her husband, Lyle, reside in a charming maritime village on the south shore of Lake Ontario in the northern Finger Lakes region of New York.

Coming Soon: *Murder at Beechwood Park*

www.ingramcontent.com/pod-product-compliance
Lightning Source LLC
Chambersburg PA
CBHW022032240626
47154CB00007B/2368